COMPULSION

The Quinn Larson Quests Book 2

P.A. WILSON

FREE EBOOK

Claim your copy of Spells and Other Charms when you use the QR code to sign up for my newsletter and learn more about Quinn and Cate's past.

CHAPTER 1

I t was only eight am, but I had been talking to Lionel for hours. He'd learned a lot since we started this apprenticeship, but today it was almost impossible for him to concentrate and I was hanging onto my last nerve. I ran my fingers gently across the ingredients laid out on the bench, testing them. The waxiness of the rind told me the lemon zest was still potent. The charcoal crumbled properly in my fingers, and when I pressed on the dried thyme the aroma filled my senses. It wasn't the ingredients. "Try it again. Start with the lemon rind."

"I'm so sorry, Quinn. I don't know what it is. Maybe there's a storm coming. But then, maybe it's me."

He had a point about the storm, but not about himself. It didn't make any sense that this little spell would trip him up. "Can you cleanse the spirits from the room?"

"Maybe."

I didn't like the tone of his voice; it was way too uncertain. I suspected he was telling me what he thought I wanted to know. Not for the first time, I wished I still had my sight. Well I could still do some things. "You're tired and it's been too long since I cast a spell. Let me do it."

I gave him a list of the ingredients I needed and asked him to sit on the corner of the couch, so I knew where he was.

I touched the first item, rosemary. I gave it a rub to release the smell; it seemed to clean the room by itself. Then I swirled the vinegar in the saucer. I felt the rest of the ingredients: Talc, blotting paper, and sandalwood incense.

I moved around the space to get my bearings. Cleansing didn't require much movement, but I would wreck it if I tripped mid-spell. I had gained some skill in living blind, but I had been careful not to push the envelope too much.

Satisfied that the space was clear of obstructions, I went back to the table.

"Spirits attending this room, hear my words." I crushed the rosemary. "Remember the way home." I swirled the vinegar then dripped some on the floor. "Clear the air." I sprinkled talc. "Hide in the powder if you must until we release you." I used the blotting paper to soak up the remaining vinegar. "Write in this dampness if you have a message." And, finally, I lit the incense. "I ask you to leave."

There was a sudden rush of air and I felt the room lighten.

"Is it clear?" Lionel called from across the room.

"I'll need you to check the blotting paper, see if there's a message."

I heard his footfalls come closer. "There is one."

That was a surprise. I hadn't had a spirit message for a long time. "Okay, tell me what it says."

"We need you. It is important."

"Great it couldn't be more cryptic. Is there anything about the writing that might help us figure out who sent it?"

"It is in red... but not blood. It is in block printing. And it has a seal at the bottom, a bunch of flowers."

Crap. Fairies again. I don't know why they seem to think I'm their personal problem solver. "I guess we'll find out the details from the fairies directly. I wonder why they thought they needed to do it that way. Maybe they didn't think we would believe it was important if it came directly from them."

"Should we go find out?"

"No, they'll find us. Now the room is clear, try the spell again."

"Okay, but wouldn't it be easier to just use the stove to boil the water for tea?"

I laughed. "Yes, but you need the practice, and it's relatively benign. Try again."

LIONEL FINALLY MANAGED TO BOIL WATER WITH MAGIC, WE steeped tea and headed upstairs for lunch. We got to the top of the stairs and I bumped into Lionel's back, a thing that had been happening fairly often.

"What now?"

"It's Princess Elizabeth." He moved again so I could get into the room.

"I have been waiting, wizard. Why have you blocked me from the work room? I need to speak with you."

I heard a note of imperiousness in her voice that reminded me a little of Fionuir. I knew she'd had three children in the months since she was released from my stasis spell, so I shouldn't have expected her to be the weak fairy I'd saved from starvation.

I said, "We were working, and I didn't want to be disturbed. Did you send a spirit to leave me a message?"

"No. I do not converse with spirits. They are unreliable."

"You are looking very well, Princess." Lionel broke into the conversation and I was glad of it. We were on the verge of a useless bickering session.

"Thank you, Lionel." Her voice took on a purring tone. "It is the children; they are good for the figure."

I felt around until I found a stool. Pulling it out, I hitched my hip onto the seat and waited while the two exchanged pleasantries. Lionel put the kettle on to make more tea, and he offered

Princess some honey. When we were all settled in, I decided it was time to get to the bottom of the problem she was going to drop in my lap. "Okay, Princess, we have had a spirit message and you obviously have something you need from me. Let's get it over with."

"Very well. Someone is stealing from us." I heard something in her voice that wasn't so arrogant. A little gasp between 'stealing' and 'us'.

"What is being stolen?"

"Among other things, our treasure is disappearing." I heard her rough tongue delicately lap at some honey.

"Just the Rose fairies?"

"No. We thought that at first, but it seems every tribe is losing a little treasure here and there."

I heard Lionel shift across from me and wondered what he was trying to communicate.

"How long has this been going on?"

"We noticed it three weeks ago." I tried to hear a clue in her voice, but there was nothing.

For someone who needed my help, she was stingy with the information. I tried to send out my senses to get a read on her. I felt moisture around her. That was unusual, I didn't think she was wet, but she might be crying. Maybe that's what Lionel was trying to say.

"And what was the 'among other things', Princess?"

"Before I tell you, let us talk about this favor between us."

Ah, the favor. I guessed she wanted to make sure she didn't build up too much debt to me. "Sure, what would you like to say?"

"I am happy to call us even on the favors if you will find out who is the thief."

"I am not sure I understand. Are you saying you will forgive a favor if I do you this one?"

"Yes. I know it is generous, but I am feeling generous."

"Princess, what favor do I owe you?" I saved her life and solved their breeding problem and somehow, I owed her?

"I forgave you for placing me in stasis."

"But Quinn saved your life," Lionel sputtered.

"I had determined I was not worthy of saving. I did not agree to owe you for my life."

I would have laughed if it didn't involve me helping her again. "And what about the babies? I solved that problem. Would you not agree we are even now?"

She sighed and I heard a hitch in her breath. She was crying.

"Are you expecting me to be in your debt, Quinn? Do I have to promise you a favor to get you to help? I did not think you so mercenary."

Nice. Fairies aren't the best negotiators I've ever known, but they aren't shy when it comes to getting a deal. When it comes down to it, they simply preferred to ignore any facts that weren't to their advantage.

"Princess, are you really going to play this game with me? You are clearly upset; I can hear your tears. You haven't told me the whole problem. I think that is because you don't trust me. Whatever the truth is, you must tell me." I waited for her to speak.

Lionel broke the silence. "Please, Princess, tell us what you want so we can help." That boy needed serious training in negotiation skills.

I turned to his voice and mouthed shut up at him. Hoping I wasn't talking through Princess.

"Quinn Larson, we are not sure if this other thing is stolen, or if they are simply disappearing."

"Tell me what is going on." I folded my arms and threw a stern look to where I thought Lionel was sitting.

She sighed again.

I waited. Lionel shifted in his seat but didn't speak. At least now I knew where he was.

I heard her lapping the honey again.

She sighed. "Very well. Along with our treasure, babies are disappearing. Only a few here and there."

"That is the first thing you should have said. Aside from the obvious, why would someone want to take your treasure? And why do you think they may not be stealing the babies who are disappearing?"

CHAPTER 2

P rincess had no answers for me, so she left with a demand that I fix the problem and stop asking stupid questions.

"Maybe we should see if Maeve can help," Lionel said as he returned from letting Princess out. I had become better at locating people by the sound they made, but I still hated being dependent on everyone. I'd asked Lionel to stop wearing his soft shoes so I could hear him move around in an effort to be less reliant on him. "You haven't collected on the favor she owes you from Fionuir's banishment."

We'd sent Fionuir into a dimensional fold to stop her from becoming Queen of the sidhe for another fifty years. It wasn't because I supported Maeve, it was because... well let's say it was the only choice.

"I was hoping to keep that favor for something important to me, not the fairies. But maybe we can get more than one piece of information if we're canny. What are you wearing?"

I heard Lionel pick at his pockets. He always kept them full of rocks, and pieces of shell, and other things that could be turned into charms. He sighed and I guessed we both needed to change before attending the sidhe court.

"Lionel, don't worry. I need to change as well. I've been in these easy to wear clothes far too long. We'll change and then head out this evening."

"The thing is... Well, I don't have clothes that would be acceptable for court. Maybe we can get someone else to escort you."

He knew I wasn't ready to walk into the court without help. I might never be ready. If I could see, I would go alone. Maeve might owe me a favor, but the sidhe weren't really loyal to anyone outside their court. "I can't have my apprentice looking shabby. I think as the master, I am responsible for food, shelter, and clothing. Is that right?"

"That's a really old-fashioned rule. Most apprentices these days have a side job so they can dress themselves."

Lionel's words came out in a huff of – well I couldn't tell if it was pride or embarrassment.

Whatever it was, I still needed him to be presentable. "Your side job is as my eyes so I will take care of your wardrobe, and I'll throw in some spending money too."

"Your teaching is more than enough."

"Cut the humble crap, Lionel. I am not susceptible to flattery." I heard him chuckle. "Let's get into something other than robes, jeans and tee-shirts will do. Then we can go shopping." I rubbed my chin and realized I was long past due for a shave. "Some personal grooming will be a good step too. We will come out of this looking good enough for the sidhe royalty and maybe suave enough to get more than just one answer out of Maeve."

SIX HOURS LATER, LIONEL AND I WERE STANDING OUTSIDE THE sidhe court. I asked him to tell me what he saw in ordinary sight, just to be certain what humans would see. It might not be important, but if Maeve was showing a different disguise than Fionuir, it would tell me something. Maeve had turned out to be a more thoughtful and intellectual queen that Fionuir. People still vied for invitations to parties at the court, but the mornings after were a little easier to take now.

"I don't know. It's the same as always; two men lounging outside a warehouse. Graffiti covering the walls."

Maeve hadn't made any changes then. "Do they look similar?"

"Yes. Let me check, with my Real Sight. Yes, it's the twins."

I had hoped that Maeve would have changed guards, but then again, maybe the twins had forgiven me for putting them to sleep so I could search the court. And maybe I would find the mythical master spell so I could cure my own blindness. "Okay, they may be still annoyed with me, so let's tread gently with them." Lionel led me to the door and said hello to the twins.

"Why do you speak for wizard Larson?" The voice came from the left, so I turned to face it.

"He doesn't speak for me. I also bid you good evening. Is it convenient for us to have an audience with Maeve?"

Lionel pulled me slightly back, but not fast enough to avoid the jab of a pike in my ribs. The other twin spoke this time, "That is Queen Maeve to you."

I nodded, hoping I was facing one or the other of the twins. "I need to speak with Queen Maeve, if she is at home in the court."

There was no answer. I whispered to Lionel, "What's happening?"

"One of the twins has gone inside. I hope it's to ask permission for us to enter, rather than to bring reinforcements."

I didn't think we'd done anything to provoke them into attacking, but you never knew with these two. I tried to reassure Lionel with a squeeze of the arm I was holding.

This time I smelled a faint scent of cloves and honey waft out of the door as the twin returned.

"The Queen will see you. Follow, and don't touch anything."

One twin walked in front of us, and the other behind. I

wondered that both guards could leave their post to escort us, but that was sidhe business and I didn't ask. "I am sorry, but I have been impolite. I do not know your names."

"You can call me Owen and my brother is Garnet." The voice came from behind.

I hoped that I would be able to see which was which when my eyes were healed. Or perhaps Lionel had noticed a difference between the two. I found it was useful to have names, not the real names – the ones with power – but the everyday names. It was hard to end a grudge when you thought of the other side as Twin One and Twin Two.

The scent of cloves and honey became stronger as we walked the hall that circled the court.

The court was home to all the Vancouver sidhe. When this group of sidhe rebelled a thousand years ago, they were exiled from Ireland and finally drifted to the West Coast. Finding a similar rainy climate, they set up court and started their politics.

From the outside, it looked like a warehouse. Behind the front door was a corridor that actually ran around the entire perimeter of the exterior wall. Inside that, like a secret room, was the court. The first floor was the public room and all the private rooms were in the six stories above. There was an entrance in the east corner to the stairs going up, and in the west corner, a hidden door that led to a tunnel that ended in Banks' Bar.

In my current state, I couldn't see the rich tapestries and ornate furniture that Fionuir had used to decorate the court, and I had searched for the amulet the last time I saw the room.

Now that Maeve was queen, I wondered if she'd redecorated. The incense was definitely a change. Fionuir had preferred the light scents of flowers. It seemed Maeve was much happier with the richer, deeper aroma of spice. I preferred Fionuir's taste in atmosphere – the only thing I preferred about her.

There were soft murmurs and the slither of silk against silk. I tugged Lionel's arm and said, "Lionel, tell me what you see. I can't do this without knowing what's going on."

"Sorry, Quinn. There are five or six other sidhe in the room. Maeve is speaking to Iain right now. I guess he managed to keep his involvement in Fionuir's plans a secret."

"Don't assume anything about sidhe politics, Lionel. Keep me updated." It helped to know we weren't facing the full court, despite the sound that still made me think there were more than a few sidhe in the room.

We waited for Maeve to deign to speak to us. No one offered us tea, or wine, or food. I think they ignored us because they were unsure of where we fit in the new world. The way we treated, and were treated by, Maeve would set the tone for wizard and sidhe relations for the next fifty years; even if that was just wizard Quinn Larson.

What felt like an hour passed before Lionel put a touch of pressure on my elbow to move me forward. "She is ready for us now," he whispered.

We walked forward and when he indicated I should stop, I took a low bow. It was my intention to show respect, I hoped Maeve was in a mood to cooperate.

"Quinn, it is good to see you." Maeve's voice was soft. "Please, let us bring you some clove tea. And sit here beside me."

Lionel guided me to a low stool and then left my side saying, "You are not going to be overheard here."

A slim cold hand placed a teacup and saucer into mine and I took a tiny sip. The clove was overwhelming, and I hoped I wouldn't have to drink the entire cup. "It is pleasant to be here too, Queen Maeve."

"I suppose you have come here for a reason. Speak up now so that we may get past business and into pleasantries."

"I am hoping you will be able to give me information on three things." I paused. I expected that she might limit what she shared with me, so I needed to ask my questions in order of importance.

"First, I hope that you have some way of reversing the blindness spell that Fionuir set on me." I know that was selfish, but I'd be much better if I had my sight.

Maeve sighed and I felt her hand touch my cheek. "I regret I cannot, Quinn. I am not able to undo her spells on others. I can only cleanse the sidhe she punished. You will need to find your cure yourself."

So much for Maeve easily paying her debt, I felt naive for thinking she would keep her word. I toyed with the idea of reminding her that she had promised to give me the answers when she was Queen but decided to leave that until I could think of a way to say it without sounding like a sulky two-year-old.

If she couldn't cure my blindness, I would need Lionel for longer than I had originally planned. I put that aside and asked, "I would also like any information you have on the demon that killed Cate." My words caught as I said her name. "I would have justice for that act."

Maeve sighed before saying, "I only have the rumors that we all heard. Well I suppose you did not hear them, otherwise..."

I swallowed the feeling that she was lying. It was entirely possible that she was, but it was just as possible she was not. "Please, the rumors would be useful."

"That day, we called all of the sidhe home because of the rumor that a summoning was underway without proper wards. We heard from our spirits that power was building. We tried to summon one of our demons, but they would not come."

I wondered how I had missed the clues. Then a memory of someone trying to tell me something was about to happen surfaced. The blood rushed from my head as I realized I could have saved her, if only I had taken a few minutes to listen. If only I hadn't been so determined to find that damn amulet. A familiar burning anger heated my body and I had no one to aim it at. No one but myself.

Realizing I was shaking, I took a deep breath and controlled my reaction. It was important to live in the present, not in the past. I would never be able to bring Cate back. I could only plan and wait for the right time for revenge. "Did someone in particular have information? Did the rumors come from a specific source?"

"No, I am sorry. You know how it is, Quinn. Whispers come from the shadows. Someone feels a shift in power. All I know is there was enough to make us come into the protections of the court that night."

I couldn't push it any further without risking her anger. "The last thing I wish to ask is about the fairies. There is someone stealing their treasure."

The sidhe queen laughed a trill of musical notes. "The fairies always seem to be losing something. But again, I must say no. It seems I am still in your debt without information to buy my way out."

The side effect of putting Fionuir into a dimensional fold was that Maeve was able to reclaim her throne. I would have happily freed Maeve from her obligation for the price of one answer. "Perhaps you can ask your court to pass on any tidbits of information if they find anything?"

Her hand touched my cheek again. "I will. And now, let us put aside this business and you and your apprentice can join us at dinner."

I accepted for two reasons. It would be rude to deprive Lionel of his first sidhe party, and the sidhe were famous for the glorious flavors of their food and wine.

TWO HOURS LATER, I SHOOK MY HEAD AT THE WHISPERED, "Trout in lime aspic." I needed a break from the food. Delicious as it was, I'd been living off simple food for months. The richness of the feast, with the constant scent of cloves, was straining my digestion.

"You are no longer hungry?" A voice came from my right. A male sidhe named... Nope, I couldn't remember.

"I have to admit that I am in need of a rest."

"Quinn, this fish is heavenly," Lionel said from my other side. "All of the food is a delight. I wish I could prepare such wonderful meals."

I smiled and turned back to the sidhe at my side. "My apprentice is new to all of this. Please allow him some license in his manners."

"There is no reason to excuse his enthusiasm. It is delightful to see someone enjoy our entertainment so wholeheartedly."

Before I could reply, a voice from across the table cut in, "It is amusing, Reagan. Such... innocence, perhaps that's the right expression."

The sneer dripped from the words. I heard Lionel take in a breath and I reached to touch his arm. "I remember when I first came here," I said. "Well I have to admit, I remember very little of the night, but I do recall that we were expected to be pleasant to each other. No matter how much alcohol is imbibed, anger sours the food. Is that not the expression?"

It was silent for a heartbeat. I kept a smile on my face, hoping that whoever this person was would take my words as peace keeping, not criticism.

"Yes," he finally responded. "Dinner is not the place to disagree."

I lifted my wine glass and saluted him before accepting a morsel of boar *ragu* over *gnocchi*.

HOURS LATER, WE WERE IN THE CORRIDOR AND WALKING towards the door when Lionel stopped and swore under his breath.

"What?" I reached into my pocket for the spells I kept there.

"Owen and Garnet are blocking our way." Lionel tried to move me back to the party, but I heard the door to the court open on a wave of laughter. "And two sidhe are now blocking our path back. But they are just standing there."

"What do you have on you that we can use in a fight?" I asked. My gut tightening, this was the first time I had to fight since Fionuir's spell took my sight.

I heard the little clicks and jingles of the various items Lionel kept in his pockets. "I have my staff and a stinging nettle ball. I don't want to throw the nettles; they'll get back into the court. Do you really think they want a fight? I thought Maeve approved of us."

I added politics to my mental curriculum for Lionel. He was too naive by half. "Not all the sidhe are happy with Maeve, but we may be able to avoid a fight. Give me a minute." I fingered the spells again. I had taken the time to mark them so I knew what they were. A stone with a small dot was for creating a flash of light. It might help, but it would leave everyone as blind as I was for about three minutes. I needed Lionel's eyes for this, so not a good choice.

Think, for crying out loud. Stop worrying about what might happen and figure out how to help now. I kept inventorying my spells. A nutshell with a hole in it would create the sound of horses, maybe good for a diversion. A lump that shifted under my fingers was a bee ball. It would be as bad as the nettle ball. I don't think Maeve would appreciate a swarm of bees filling the building. There was one more, a seashell that would cause a howling wind. I could contain that in the corridor.

The seconds were slipping past and no one had said anything. I banished the last doubts about my ability to fight, and whispered, "Okay between us we have two staffs, a spell that will sound like horses charging and one that will blow everything down. I guess we might have to throw a few punches." I heard Lionel's staff bang as he bounced it on the floor. I made a quick decision and said, "Point me at the twins. I should be able to keep pushing forward. You'll need to deal with whoever is behind."

Lionel turned me to face the front door and I felt his back align with mine. He cleared his throat before speaking, "They are closing in, Quinn."

I needed to get them talking first. The only way I could tell where they were was by sound. "Owen, what is this all about? We were just about to leave."

"Oh, do not fret, Quinn Larson. You will be leaving. But first we'll have a little fun." I focused on the sound of his voice and heard a slight chuckle coming from beside him. Both twins were within a few feet of me.

I heard a swish and managed to lift my staff in time to block a swipe of a pike. "Now that's not necessary, Owen. Why don't you let us pass and perhaps Maeve won't need to know about this?"

He snickered. "You think Maeve will care that we dent you a little?"

I couldn't tell where Garnet was, so I swept my staff out in a curve to judge my clearance. I heard the sound of shoes sliding on stone – one of the twins dodged my sweep.

Lionel grunted and then moved away from my back. I heard the sound of a scuffle coming from behind but knew I had to deal with Owen. He was the ringleader. If I could take him down, the others would stop fighting – I hoped.

"Owen, it's not necessary for you to do this. I promise we can settle our differences at some point. I just think it would be more honorable if you waited until I could see you."

There was no answer. Then I heard the swish again. I ducked and felt the air move above me. If that had connected it would have done more than just dent me a bit. Then a pike jabbed me in the side. Thank the spirits that it was the blunt end.

I heard Lionel start to mutter behind me and the sound of a staff making contact with flesh. I hoped it was sidhe flesh.

I sensed movement to my right and swung my staff in an arc

to stop whatever attack was coming. I made contact with an arm. I heard it snap and one of the twins screamed in pain. Maybe that would bring someone from the court to the rescue. But no, I remembered that this corridor was created to keep the sounds from the street away from the court.

"I apologize for that," I said. "If only I could see, I would have aimed better."

Lionel was muttering louder now, and I realized he was preparing a spell. That almost worried me more than the attacking sidhe. I only had one to deal with, but I didn't know where he was. There was no sound other than the moaning ahead of me, and the fight behind.

Then Lionel's voice rose to a roar and I felt the sharp edge of a pike scratch my shoulder and then fall away.

"Come on," Lionel grabbed my arm and started running.

CHAPTER 3

"**W**hat spell was that?" I asked as soon as we were far enough away from the court to stop.

"Well, I wasn't sure if anything I cast would affect you, so I cast a spell of blindness. Is that okay?"

"What? You blinded four sidhe? I don't think Maeve will let that go." I hadn't taught him that spell. What else was he hiding?

"Cate taught it to me. It's one of the four defensive spells. I guess you can't do it because of being a spirit wizard, the 'do no harm' part of your vow." He stopped panting. "Good thing I'm an air. Being able to do some harm can come in handy. I don't like it though; it feels like cheating. Anyway, their blindness isn't permanent. They probably have their sight back already."

"Probably?" I couldn't figure out a way to check right now, so I had to hope for the best until I could get someone to find out if there were four blind sidhe. My spirit vow wasn't the whole of it. I'd taken an obligation to Fionuir that I couldn't cause harm to a sidhe. I was pretty sure that covered any harm Lionel did. And I'm sure that it still stood even though she wasn't around to enforce it. No use in trying to undo it. "At least we got away without too much damage. Or did we? You sound all right, are you?"

"I'm fine." He touched my shoulder. "Your suit is ripped where they got you with the pike."

I wasn't ready to go home. The buzz I had from the wine at dinner was a dim memory and I wanted to feel and hear people around me. "How about a beer? Banks' can't be far away."

"It's down this block, but aren't you afraid that the sidhe will come through the tunnel?" Lionel started leading me despite his words.

The tunnel between the sidhe court and Banks' Bar was where I'd lost my sight. "I don't think so. One of the twins has a broken arm and I guess they are trying to explain that to Maeve right now." I chuckled. "You did a good job on that spell. Congratulations."

Lionel coughed and I knew his face was getting red. "Thanks, I didn't really think about it. I just did it."

Before I could try to boost his confidence anymore, he pulled me to a stop and I heard the noise from inside Banks' flow out of the door.

Banks' was the bar for the Real Folk in Vancouver. Like most Real Folk places, it looked different from the outside. The humans were too curious to let them see something interesting. Most humans wouldn't notice it. It was just a metal door in Trounce Alley, looking like it led to a drug den. Inside it was warm, noisy, and smelled like a real bar; beer, food, and just a faint trace of smoke.

I heard Mark, the owner and bartender, call my name and started towards the sound.

"Hey, Quinn," he said, his voice rumbling. "You look like you've been through the wringer. Isn't your apprentice keeping you out of trouble?"

I heard the tap of a glass on the counter in front of me and reached for the drink before answering. A sip of the whiskey gave me a minute to find an answer that wouldn't give away too much. "Give Lionel one of these on my tab. He pulled me out of a bit of a situation tonight."

Mark grunted and I heard Lionel say thanks, and then he started coughing. Mark laughed. "I think we need to train him up to the good stuff, Quinn."

"No, I think it's better for him to start with the good stuff. At least until he has to pay for his own drinks."

I'd given Mark an anti-smoke spell a couple of months ago, and he paid me with free drinks. The spell allowed people inside Banks' to smoke whatever they wanted because it absorbed the fumes, and nothing escaped through the door to the street. Since Vancouver was a no smoking in public places city, we couldn't take the chance some human would report a smell of smoke.

"You know, Quinn," Lionel said before the whiskey took his voice again. I waited until he cleared his throat and started talking. "Maybe we can get some information from someone in here. The room's pretty full."

"Tell me who's here." I tried to think whom we could ask about the fairies' problem. Other fairies would be about as helpful as Princess, but there were Folk who knew a lot of secrets.

"There's only a few people I know. Burr and Sting are drinking with a kobold I am pretty sure I haven't seen before."

It was hard to tell the kobolds apart if you weren't used to them. All those hard spikes sticking out of their body kind of distracted you from the odd facial feature.

The two fairies had been useful when we got the amulet back from Fionuir so we could reverse the spell that stopped them breeding. "I don't know. If the fairies knew anything they would be coming to tell us. They'll all know Princess got us involved."

Lionel grunted his agreement. I assumed it was because he'd taken another sip. After a second he said, "Beacon is sitting alone at a table, what about him? He's got lots of connections."

That was a good idea. Beacon was a sprite and they were

everywhere. Beacon, in particular, was connected through his cousins to half the sprites in town, and by friendship to ninety percent of the other Real Folk.

"Get Mark to pour us a round and whatever Beacon is drinking. We'll go over and talk."

"Um, Quinn, would it be okay if mine was a cider? I don't think I can drink another of these for a while."

Mark said he'd drop off the round in a minute, so Lionel led me to a table that was on the back wall, if my sense of direction was right.

"Can we join you, or would you prefer your solitude?" I asked, knowing full well a sprite would rather have company.

"As long as you don't bring trouble, Quinn Larson. I have no desire to be on the wrong side of the sidhe, or any other being for that point." His voice was warm and full.

"I never intend to bring trouble," I said.

Beacon laughed at that. Lionel put my hand on the back of a chair and left me to seat myself. The drinks arrived and we took our first sips in silence.

"The fairies are having problems again," Beacon said. "I suppose they came to you."

"Yes, but why would you think that?" I was happy that he'd brought up the subject, but not so happy that he'd made the assumption.

"You are getting a reputation for being the fairies' go-to guy." He laughed again and I'm not sure if it was at me, or with me. "The last time you got involved, you paid a terrible price, but didn't take it out on them."

Apparently, Beacon had never tried to reason with a fairy. "I don't seem to have any choice. You know what the problem is?"

"I do, but I have no information for you. I don't have any desire to get involved with their problems. You already know how difficult it is to walk away when you do get involved."

I heard Lionel's chair scrape. He'd been quiet up to now, but he usually didn't have a lot of patience. I waited to see if he would speak, but after a moment of silence I decided he had come to his senses.

"Can I get you another drink?" I still wasn't ready to go home and hoped that we'd get a hint of news about the twins before we had to go.

"You can buy me another drink, and maybe I do have other information for you. I assume you are still trying to find out who brought the demon that killed Cate."

"I am." I felt the familiar burn of rage at the mention of Cate's death. This time I had to suppress the tiny light of hope his words raised.

"I might have a clue."

I sent Lionel for more drinks before I said, "Beacon, please remember that Lionel also lost his teacher that night. If you can just be plain with your information it would help. When he is upset, he loses control over the spells."

"And you are not upset?" His surprise came through his voice.

"I am." The understatement of the century. If I could just do as I wanted, I'd...Well I didn't want to think about what I'd do. "The difference between me and Lionel is that I've learned control. I do not wish to live through another miscasting of a spell. At least until I can see."

"I get it, I won't upset him. I lost a good friend that night; don't think I'm not feeling the loss." Beacon mumbled a thanks and Lionel exchanged my empty glass for a full one. This time it was beer.

"So," Lionel said, his voice cracking slightly. "What is your clue?"

I heard Beacon take a long slurp of his beer and then place the glass heavily on the table. "I trust that you will continue to exercise control and not act without considering the consequences." He paused until I swore I would be careful. "It is rumored that there is a coven in the city."

"Great." I sighed. The only groups that called themselves covens were humans who thought they were mages. "I thought you meant a real clue."

Beacon laughed again, his sprite humor never too far from the surface. "I know, they never really have any power, but this rumor says that this coven is different. And they were planning on raising a demon that same night that Cate was killed."

Humans.

I did not want to deal with humans. It was bad enough that I lost Cate and my sight trying to stop the fairies from killing humans, now I was going to have to track down some and stop them from trying to do magic. "I still think it's not possible for humans to raise a demon. But it might be something to follow up on."

"Has there never been a human capable of doing magic?" Lionel asked.

I forgot how shallow his experience was, he'd been doing his best before he found Cate to teach him, but he'd only been with her for a month or two before she was killed. Most apprentices were given hours of history research, but Cate seems to have jumped right into spell casting. "The humans have all kinds of legends and myths, but even the druids have been unable to prove anything."

"There are a lot of stories floating around, but when you try to get details it always comes to nothing," Beacon added. "I guess it's possible, but not really probable."

Lionel started tapping his fingers on the table beside me. It was an annoying habit, but at least I knew where he was when he did it. I heard a sigh, and then he asked, "What if the demon made it happen? I mean what if the demon wasn't really summoned, but just arrived?"

Beacon laughed and then stopped. "Sorry, I know you weren't joking, but can you imagine a world where demons could just come and go as they please?"

"Demons can't enter our world without being summoned," I said.

I figured we had time for a quick lesson, and it would help if Lionel understood the basics, since he'd need to be my eyes on this. "Demons come in two types. Ones who want to be left alone and ones who want to come here and wreak havoc. We tend to get information from the ones who want to be left alone. They always bargain for payment, but really they give the information so they can go back to where they come from."

"Like Ranseed? But I thought he was a spirit," Lionel said.

I took a sip of my beer. It was difficult for some wizards to feel comfortable with the vast gray areas in magical ethics. "Okay, so you like Ranseed and he is a spirit. The thing is, we don't like to think we're doing business with demons. To make it sound better we call the ones we get information from spirits. It's not that much of a stretch. The important part is that the real demons are the evil ones; the ones that destroy for fun."

It was quiet at the table. Not being able to see what was going on in Lionel's mind from the cues on his face could mean I handled this all wrong. This kind of information could set him on a different path; I had friends who became hermits rather than deal in the gray areas.

Beacon finally filled the silence. "I think he's okay, Quinn. At least he hasn't fainted or anything."

Before I could speak, Lionel started talking. "Yes, I am fine with it. I think so anyway. So, the ones that are demons, for the sake of clarity let's keep to the demons and spirits, for the demons, there's no way they can enter our world without help. So why would you summon a demon?"

That was a hard one. I had never understood the fascination with demons. Yes, they can give you quick results, but the price was always more than the results were worth. "Desperation."

Beacon grunted. "Yes, and fear, maybe. Nothing good ever comes of it no matter what you tell yourself. I'm glad we sprites don't have that kind of magic. Temptation can make fools of us all. Fools with magic are dangerous. As Cate found out."

We sipped our drinks for a while keeping our thoughts private. I listened to the buzz of the conversation, but nothing rose out of the babble to capture my interest.

"Another round?" Mark's voice came through the fog of my thoughts. I said yes. Lionel said to make his tea, which was my cue that he thought I'd need a lot of help getting home.

"I've been thinking. There is one other possibility," Lionel said when Mark had placed the new drinks on the table.

"What's that?" Beacon asked.

"They aren't human. Is there any chance a wizard child grew up as a human?"

I didn't even have to give that a thought. "No, we don't exchange babies. If a wizard child went missing, we'd find it."

Lionel ignored me. "It would have to be a witch or a wizard. A sprite or a fairy, or anyone else would look wrong, not human at all."

"I said no." I reached out to touch his arm. My voice had been louder than I intended. I leaned forward and whispered, "I am sorry. I know you are looking for reasons here, but there aren't any reasons."

Beacon tapped the table before Lionel could try to argue. "I think we need to go before you attract too much attention."

"We can keep it down," Lionel said. "I think we should consider the possibility."

"You need to give Lionel some research tasks, Quinn," Beacon said. "I don't think he's going to believe you without following up on the histories himself."

I started to argue, but then realized he was right. I wouldn't have given up on a good idea when I was that age. I still wouldn't, but I think my ideas are better these days.

Lionel took my arm without speaking and led me to the door.

I heard Beacon following us. "I'll walk with you for a bit," he said. "I need some air."

We stood outside the door cooling off for a minute before leaving the alley. I turned to thank Beacon for the information, and something flicked my cheek. It felt sharp and gentle at the same time.

"The Morrigan," Lionel gasped. "Are you okay? She touched you."

I ran my hands across my cheek, no blood. I didn't feel any sudden metamorphosis either, so it wasn't like when she touched Olan and turned him from pixie to chickadee. "I think so. Still blind, but other than that I'm okay. Where is she?"

"Perched on a window ledge," Beacon answered. "She's just watching us."

I looked up at where I remembered the ledge was. I didn't have much patience with her games, so I shouted, "What do you want, Morrigan?"

She cawed, it sounded like a thousand ghosts crying. It stopped my words in my throat and left me deaf to all but a hollow wind.

Then the sound came back and I heard Lionel whisper," She's gone."

"Yes, but look at this." Beacon gave my arm a gentle tug. "It's a coin. Sorry, here."

He put the coin in my hand and I felt fairies, and something else. "Is this all?"

Lionel let my go of my arm. "Just a second, there's something caught here."

I rubbed the coin between my fingers while I waited. This was definitely fairy gold. I could feel their energy pulsing through the metal.

"Beacon, can you give me a boost?" Lionel's voice was strained.

I felt Beacon leave my side and then heard him grunt. "You might be skinny, wizard, but you are certainly not light."

"Got it." I heard a second grunt and Lionel returned to my side. "It's a bit of fabric, but it's weird. Like it's silk but thick and not as slippery."

I held out my hand, but Beacon spoke before Lionel gave me the scrap. "Nymph."

That explained the feeling of the something else on the coin, but it didn't make sense. Why would a nymph steal fairy gold?

CHAPTER 4

"I know a few nymphs," Beacon said. "Let me have a good look at the cloth." I held it out for him. "Not much here but leave it with me and I'll see if I can get some information for you."

"We'll come along," I said. I didn't want to trust that Beacon would be able to leave the park if he went in. Sprites had to spend time taking care of the health of the plants. If Beacon got caught up in that, we'd wait until next week for him to come out.

We headed to Stanley Park where most of the city's nymphs lived. It was still early enough that Real Folk would be out and about in the park, and late enough that there would be very few humans.

When I could see, I loved this walk. Now I just kept a memory of the changes in the environment in my mind. Warehouses and old stores giving way to newer buildings, stores, financial buildings, and finally high-rises; block after block of glass and concrete, then nature. The park was on a blob of land that jutted out into Burrard Inlet. It was home to all manner of trees, plants, and Real Folk. I thought of it as a garden surrounded by a forest.

Some of the trees were a thousand years old and were almost as smart as the rest of the Folks.

"Can you manage a bit of rough ground?" Beacon asked. "We'll have the best luck on the far side of the lagoon."

"If we don't go too fast, I'll be okay. And anyway, if I fall over, I'm sure you will pick me up."

We slipped through a gap in the trees and made our way towards the lagoon. The damp scent of fallen leaves and a heaviness of humidity wrapped itself around me.

The path was narrow enough that I had to walk behind Beacon with my hand on his shoulder for guidance. I still felt the brush of trees as I passed. I was sure that without Beacon this path would have been invisible. Sprites have secret ways and means in the forest.

I stumbled a few times along the way but managed not to fall. When I heard the sound of the fountain in the middle of Lost Lagoon, I relaxed. Our trip was almost complete.

"There's a space over here where you can wait while I go find a nymph." Beacon placed me against a tree trunk that was so wide I couldn't feel around it.

I lowered myself to the ground and settled in. Lionel sat beside me. I could feel him start to fidget as soon as Beacon's footsteps faded away.

I was tired. The party and then the fight, after a night of little sleep, were starting to catch up with me; making me more irritated than usual with his activity. When I had control of my annoyance, I asked, "What?"

"I just started reading about nymphs yesterday. So why did we have to come here to wait? Why couldn't Beacon just bring a nymph to the path?"

The best way for him to learn was to think through his own answers. "How far did you get in your research?"

He sighed; a sound I was getting used to hearing. "I only managed the first page before we headed out to get ready to see

Maeve. So, I know they have habitats in trees, and water, and they take on the appearance of where they live." He paused and smacked his lips together while he thought. "And they are tied to their homes. Okay. So, we need to be near the water because Beacon thinks it's a water nymph."

"Good thinking. And what else does that tell you?"

"I guess I'm having difficulty understanding how a nymph would be able to stay away from its home long enough to steal treasure."

He had a good mind when he took the time to use it. "Yep. So, there's more to this story than we think."

"Okay, so we – Oh, you scared me almost out of my skin. Where did you come from?"

"What's going on?" I felt for my charms hoping to find a defensive spell.

Lionel touched my arm to stop me reacting. "A fairy just popped out of the ground."

Before I could say anything, a piping voice broke the silence. "You are Quinn Larson."

"Yes. If you know that then you know I can't see you. Who are you?"

I felt a tiny hand touch mine. She was one of the very wee Folk. "I am Selencia of the clover clan. I come to tell you that we are grateful you are going to find our babies."

"I will do my best." Never make a promise to the wee Folk. They were mean if they thought you lied to them.

"You will do it. You helped us make babies and now you will save them. I have a gift for you." She tugged at my fingers so I turned my hand over. "This spell will give you back your sight for one hour. You swallow it and in ten minutes you will be able to see."

She put a nutshell in my hand. I thanked her and said, "I am not sure I can swallow something so large."

A tinkling of bells came as she laughed. "The spell is inside, silly wizard. It is a seed; you will be able to swallow it without water. The shell is just to protect it from loss."

"If I may ask, Selencia," Lionel said. "What did you use to make the spell? It would be very useful if Quinn could cure his blindness for more than an hour."

"You may always ask, apprentice, but I cannot tell you the clan secret. Even if I could, you would not be able to use it. If the wizard swallowed more than two of these spells in a year, he would die."

There was always a catch. Even in wizard magic, spells only took you so far, and some of the really useful ones are so complicated it takes years to learn them and gather the ingredients. "I thank you for your kindness, Selencia of the clover clan." The resentment I felt was unfair. She'd given me a gift. It wasn't her fault I was blind.

"She's already gone, Quinn."

I slipped the nutshell into my pocket. The thing was, knowing that I could change my situation for even an hour made the blindness worse. Lionel shifted beside me, sending off little crinkles and crackles as he crushed leaves beneath him.

"It shouldn't be too long." I hoped I was right. I could feel the dampness seeping into my joints. "Beacon won't stay away long."

"I wasn't worried about that. I was wondering if you could trust the spell Selencia gave you." He slapped at something and suddenly I was aware of the mosquitoes clouding around us.

"It should be fine. She gave it as a thank you, so it would shame her to trick me." I slapped at a tickle on my arm.

"Is there anything we can do to make sure?"

I didn't know why he was so worried. "We can run a quick scan spell to see if there is any danger floating around it. But I will put money on the fact it's good." Money, and all my hopes.

"Oh, hi," Lionel said.

Before I could remind him to tell me, Beacon answered, "This is Dirant. He's a wood imp. We got to chatting and I think he has some information for you."

A wood imp? That was good. They were into everything including humans. As long as there was a tree, or mature shrub, within a short walk, they could do anything. And in Vancouver there were trees everywhere.

I considered my words. We didn't want Dirant to pick up any information. Wood imps couldn't be trusted with a secret; they'd talk to anyone with the patience to listen. "What about your original target?"

Beacon huffed. "No one is about right now. We'll have to try again."

Lionel was being quiet. I hoped he was listening to everything and filing it away for future questions.

"It is good to meet you, Quinn Larson. I hear you are a wise and generous wizard." Dirant's words came out scratchy, like he'd swallowed a mouthful of leaves.

"What would you like as payment?"

"I would only wish a favor, something you will pay in the future," Dirant said.

"I will not kill anyone for you. I will not steal anything, and I don't do love potions. What kind of favor does that leave?"

Dirant wheezed a laugh out. "Ah yes, you are smart. I think we can agree that the favor will not violate any oaths you have given. And will not cost you more than you will be willing to pay."

That was as good as it got with a wood imp. But he would probably just want some information to sell on anyway, so I agreed.

He rubbed his hands together in a dry scratching sound. "There are rumors floating around that a nymph is in trouble."

I nodded. It didn't pay to talk too much with the wood imps. They were easily distracted. And if they got off on some tangent, you could wait all day for them to get back to the point.

"Did you know that a family of nymphs arrived with the new

trees the humans planted? It seems that they came from Asia. Some place very far away. I had never heard of it. Have you?"

I felt Lionel take a breath and jabbed him with my elbow so he wouldn't engage.

"I was trying to get a look at the new nymphs. I like to know about any change in the population of the forest. I saw three females, very pretty. And there was one male, but he was old and wrinkled."

I clenched my teeth around a yawn. This was going to take a while.

"And I saw something very different. You know that nymphs stay close to home. If they are tied to a lake they can go as far as the highest water line. The sea nymphs have more freedom of course. But ones attached to trees can't move farther than the longest reach of the roots."

I nodded for Dirant to continue.

"So, these new ones – they are blue and kind of like the inside of the shell, iridescent. Anyway, I was just watching and wondering how I could help them settle in. I like to be helpful you know. I thought maybe I could bring them some supplies. From places they couldn't go, you know. Like maybe some water from the lagoon for their trees. And then the old one started tying leaves in the hair of the females. When he was done, he whispered something and they left. They went way farther than the roots of their trees. After all, the trees were just planted, and the roots would still be in a ball. I slipped under the soil to check. I swear those nymphs were spying."

He stopped to take in a gulp of air, and I held up my hand. "This is good information. Can you describe the nymphs? Were they wearing clothes, for instance?"

"No, they weren't. Is that important?"

I didn't share the news that we'd found the scrap of clothing. "I don't know. What else can you tell me about them?"

"Let me think."

We waited. Imps had photographic memories. It was probably why they sold information – it was easily storable and retrievable and didn't need to be hauled around.

"I went to the trees to see them and then I saw what I said, and then I watched them go. Oh yes, they were carrying bags. The bags were made of the usual nymph material. It was gray-green and like skin."

I would have to get confirmation on the color, but 'like skin' was a good description of the feel of the scrap of fabric.

"Can you show us where they are?" I might not be able to see, but if we got close, I might be able to sense something.

"Beacon knows. And they are gone now anyway. You should go back tomorrow, or later."

The cold had numbed anything remotely touching the earth, and I wanted to get home to process this information before we did anything else. "Is there anything more you think we should know?"

"No. How do I get in touch with you to collect my favor?"

I picked up a bit of bark from the ground and muttered a calling spell over it. "When you need me, break this and say where and when you want to meet. I'll hear it and come."

Dirant picked the bark off my hand and said his goodbyes. Beacon said he had someplace to be and I asked Lionel to lead me home.

"I think we should at least go look at the new trees before we go home," Lionel said, while leading me back down the path to the road. "What can it hurt?"

I kept my focus on following the movement of his body. I could feel when he had to step over something and when the ground changed, but it didn't tell me when a tree might slap me in the face, or when a rock might turn.

"We'll discuss it when we are back on firm footing," I said through clenched teeth.

He sighed and moved a little faster.

I tightened my grip on his shoulder and tried to pull back. "Lionel, slow down a bit; getting out of here in one piece is better than getting out fast."

I didn't catch what he said, but his pace slowed a little and I was able to follow him out of the forest without twisting an ankle or tripping over anything. By the sounds, we came out near Lumbermen's Arch. I asked Lionel to hold on while I caught my breath. It wasn't the physical exercise that had me panting, it was concentrating. At least, that was what I told myself.

"I'm sorry, Quinn." Lionel's voice also came out on heavy breathing. "I sometimes forget that you can't see. I mean... I don't forget you are blind, but when it's dark, like now, and I can't see all that well... I kind of forget you can't see at all."

"Don't worry, Lionel. No harm no foul. Look is there anyone around?" I figured it was about two in the morning by now. It would be unusual for anyone to be hanging around here; unusual but not impossible.

"Not a soul in sight." He touched my elbow, our signal that he was ready to move when I was. "If we are going home, we should start off now. It's not that far, but it feels like rain's coming."

"We'll come back and you can check out the new nymphs another time. If it's that dark, you won't see anything."

He patted my elbow again. "I know, I didn't think about that when we were sitting with Beacon and Dirant. You know, the sprites and imps glow a bit at night. I didn't realize how much difference it made."

We started walking toward my house. I live just behind St. Paul's Hospital. The hospital made a great landmark, but the noise of the ambulances on some nights made it difficult to study. But having a house in that neighborhood, one with a garden for my herbs and a full basement for my workshop, was worth a little noise pollution.

"I could go back at sunrise," Lionel suggested. "I don't need much sleep, and you don't need to come. I could be in and out before they even have a chance to notice me."

"I need to be there in case anything goes wrong." I was not going to let him get caught by some strange nymphs; particularly nymphs who seem a little too mobile.

"We could spend some time figuring out where the trees are, and I could just go look."

"Lionel, I said no." I tried to fill my voice with all the command of a master to his apprentice. I am not sure it worked, but Lionel stopped arguing for a couple of blocks.

"What about tomorrow at sunset? I know there are a lot of humans who run around the seawall in the evening, but we should be able to pass until we head into the forest."

It was my turn to sigh. "Look, I know you're curious. And I know it's a solid lead for the fairies. But I need to do some research on these teenagers first. The fairy problem comes second."

He came to a halt and I almost knocked him over when I walked into his back.

"Lionel, what's wrong?" I fingered the spells in my pocket, ignoring the temptation to swallow the sight one, looking for something defensive.

"Nothing." He started walking again.

I tugged his elbow to make him stop. "Nothing? Really?"

"Well nothing dangerous. I just thought we were going to help Princess out."

"We have information to follow about the demon. We'll help Princess, but I am putting the fairies second."

Lionel started walking again. "But this lead on the nymphs is hot. We have nothing definite on the teenagers."

I let the subject lie until we were home. I could almost feel the frustration radiating off my apprentice. I was hoping he would figure it out himself. It was good training for him to do that.

Lionel couldn't rely on me to always be there. He needed to be able to face reality.

We had washed up and were sitting at the table sipping mint tea before he spoke again.

"I am trying to understand, Quinn. But I can't think why you aren't going to follow up on what Dirant told us."

"Look what happened the last time I put the fairies first. I lost Cate, and I lost my sight." I pushed the mug away. "I don't have much else to lose."

CHAPTER 5

The next morning, we sat over a breakfast of thick oatmeal with dried cherries and coconut. I have to admit that my eating habits had vastly improved since Lionel moved in. I guess there are benefits to having an apprentice around after all.

I finished my coffee and decided it was time to start planning our next steps. "You don't happen to have any contacts that would know about the humans?" I asked Lionel.

"I barely have any contacts in the Real Folks, let alone contacts who know humans. We all pretty much avoid them," Lionel said over the sound of the dishes he was clearing. "If we are going to try to track down the human teenagers, the information is going to come from your contacts. How about calling a spirit or two?"

"That's not a bad idea." I had been thinking over our conversation from the night before. As much as I wanted to concentrate on getting revenge, the fairies would never let me put them second. I had to deal with both problems at the same time. "You know, we could split our resources. If you go into the park and find out more about the nymphs, I could do the research on the humans."

He didn't answer.

"Lionel? I thought you were hot to follow that lead?" Still no answer. "Are you still in the room?"

"Sorry. Yes, I do think we should go investigate the nymphs. But how are you going to do anything if I'm not here to help?" His voice was tight.

"I'm not completely helpless. If you make sure I set the circle before you leave, I should be able to summon a spirit or two and ask some questions. Or, we could call Beacon. Or Clarence."

"Clarence is on his honeymoon."

I remembered that: Prague.

It was much harder for Real Folk like kobolds, and even sprites, to move around during the day when the humans were all over the place. But with the right charm, and a bit of stealth, it could be done. A wizard or witch looked pretty much like a human, so I usually didn't give it much thought.

"I can go find Beacon, though," Lionel offered after a moment. He still sounded like there was something unsaid. But I didn't want to demand an answer.

I thought of another solution. "Or I could use the sight spell from Selencia."

"No," his answer was sharp and sudden. "You need to use that for something more important than just getting along without me. If you think it's more important to follow the humans, then we should do that."

If I waited, I'd be an old man before he told me what was bothering him. "What's going on? If I'm such a bad mentor that you are afraid to tell me something then—"

"No, you're a great mentor." I felt him sit beside me. "You are right. I just... I am worried that... No. I'm just being selfish."

Light dawned, figuratively. "You are afraid that I don't need you."

This time his sigh carried relief rather than frustration. "You agreed to take me on until you could manage on your own. I want you to regain your sight, but I also want to stay on as your apprentice."

"I won't throw you out on the street." I tried to find words that would reassure him without binding me to a promise. "Look, you're a good student. I can't guarantee what will happen in the future, any more than you can. But until I get my sight back, we are mentor and apprentice. We'll work something out when it changes. You just need to worry about your studies and your prac- tice." And I needed to start becoming more independent, so Lionel got more training out of me.

"Okay, but Quinn?"

"What?"

"I really do want you to be able to see again."

Now it was going to get mushy if I didn't change the subject. "I know. Look we can still do both. If you and I talk through everything, and we get set up right, it will work."

We spent most of the morning going through the nymph lore I had, trying to find any reference to foreign nymphs. My library was focused on the west coast beings because I didn't go very global in my research. New Real Folk occasionally moved into the area, but often kept to themselves.

"So, I should be observing everything and not making assump- tions," Lionel said.

"I think you need to make sure you don't offend the nymphs based on what we know about our type. So, no touching, no looking in their eyes, don't ask for names, but if they offer, give them yours without hesitation."

He nodded. "I'll try to seek for Dirant when I get into the trees. I know what direction he pointed, and we know where the old trees were standing, so I shouldn't have too much trouble locating the new ones."

"Write everything in that notebook I gave you. I'm told your drawing skill is more than passable. If you can draw each nymph so we – I mean you and Beacon – can look for distinguishing marks."

I heard him flip through the pages of the book. "I'm as ready as I can be. We just need to wait for midday to pass. Unless they are very different, the nymphs won't leave the tree until the sun starts to drop."

I nodded. He was right, there was such a thing as over-planning. The truth was that as soon as he walked away from me the plans could go completely sideways.

"Quinn, what are you going to do?"

"This evening I'm going to Banks'. But I want to walk through the park with you this afternoon. I think you'll have much better luck with the nymphs in the evening. If we see who's around after lunch, maybe we'll get some information that will help later."

THERE'S A SPACE BETWEEN ONE AND THREE WHEN THE PARK IS – maybe not empty, but the humans who are there are peaceful. There are more mothers with young children than joggers, skateboarders, and bicyclists. There's a sleepy feeling that is perfect if you want to wander the nooks and crannies. Humans mainly stayed on the paved ways. There were a few who had put up tents and lived in the shadows of the centuries-old trees, but most were wary of the violence they imagined lurked in the world off the trails.

I told Lionel where to slip onto a Real Folk trail so we wouldn't be noticed. I didn't need to be able to see that we had entered it. The temperature dropped about ten degrees and the humidity rose by twenty percent.

"We're in far enough that no one will hear us," Lionel said, guiding me to a rock that was large and had a flat top. "I'm not clear on why we aren't just going to go straight to the new trees. The nymphs will be there."

I picked out the contents of the bag I was holding and laid them on the top of the rock before speaking. "I am a hindrance. I'll make noise stumbling about and they might just hide."

"Okay." He flicked a lighter, the windproof kind. I'd had him carry the lighter because I carried some pretty volatile ingredients. "Aren't you worried that you'll call one of them here?"

"I've thought of that, but it's a good point." That felt weird, like I was telling him he was stupid and smart in the same sentence. "I mean, you are getting better at thinking things through."

He stumbled over his thanks and then went to gather some moss and pinecones. While I waited, I organized the ingredients on the table; rosemary at twelve o'clock, lemon rinds at three o'clock, cinnamon at six o'clock. I was glad I hadn't lost my sense of smell too. The rest of the positions were for the moss, and pinecones, and the powder I kept in my pocket. I heard Lionel galumphing through the undergrowth and despaired about his ability to sneak up on the nymph camp.

"Are these what you wanted?" he asked, placing a variety of bits and pieces in my hand.

"Yes." I placed them in position as I spoke. "Can you be quieter later? When you are alone?"

"I made noise so you would know I was coming," he said.

"I appreciate it, but practice being quiet and don't worry about me." I closed my eyes − I know, but it helped me concentrate − and ran through the spell before I sprinkled on the fire powder. It would need to be perfect; mistakes couldn't be fixed.

I finally pulled out the twist of paper holding the fine powder. "Lionel, are you ready?"

"I am." He took the paper from me and I heard the crinkle of it untwisting. "Are you going to talk me through it?"

I nodded.

"I'm standing centered on the cinnamon. Let me clear my

mind." I heard a long hiss of air as he breathed out any thoughts. "Ready."

"Sprinkle the powder widdershins from six o'clock all the way. When you are done, make a line of powder to the center and pour out the remainder in a pile."

I heard the hiss of the power sliding against paper. "Done."

"Remember to keep in your mind the beings we are calling as the four symbols burn. Lemon for imp, rosemary for—"

"Quinn, I know; rosemary for pixie, cones and moss for sprite, and cinnamon for wood fairy."

I shut up and let him finish the spell. I heard the lighter flick and when the last hiss and crackle of the burning powder faded, we waited. It could take up to an hour for someone to respond. It all depended on who was near.

"Here we go," Lionel whispered.

"Why did you call me?" A voice I recognized.

"Hello, Dirant." I hoped we hadn't wasted our spell on him. "I am sorry we interrupted whatever you were doing. We were trawling for information on the new arrivals."

"I don't have anything new for you. I have been watching them on and off, and they haven't done anything else surprising." His voice carried no irritation. I think he was enjoying his role as informant.

"Could you take me there later?" Lionel blurted out his question and I wondered what Dirant would expect in return if he agreed.

"You won't like it in there. It's cold and dirty," Dirant said.

I let Lionel do the talking. He needed to learn how to negotiate and I could always pull him out of any situation a wood imp created.

"I don't mind that," Lionel said, his voice casual. "Wouldn't it be nice to have a bit of company?"

Dirant tsked. "You might scare them away. You are very large."

"No, I promise I will be as silent as you need me to be." Lionel was doing well. He'd managed to avoid any opening for Dirant to grab a favor.

"You must promise not to talk to them," Dirant whispered. "I do not think they want to talk to anyone."

"I promise," Lionel whispered back. "I will just observe."

"I'm heading there in a couple of hours. I can take you. Meet me in the rose garden. Bring candy. Bye."

"Well better than nothing," I said. "You need a bit of practice, but you did okay."

"Thanks. I tried," Lionel said. "What should I have done better?"

I had to remember to be careful when I gave Lionel praise. I hadn't meant to criticize. "We can talk about it later when you can tell me how far you would have gone to get him to agree."

He sighed. "I probably should have just offered candy to start with."

"What can you expect from an imp?" a thin high voice said. A wood fairy had come.

"Thank you for joining us." I smiled; it was best to be polite to fairies in their habitat. "We wonder if you have seen the new tree Folk."

"Yes, they are odd. I do not like odd people," she said, dismissing the topic. "Is there something else you would like to know, or can I go?"

Interesting, I wasn't going to let it go that easily. "What makes them so odd?"

She sniffed. "They do not speak to us. They move around too much. They are odd."

I guess my first instinct was wrong, this was not jealousy; it was disinterest. We were not going to get much more. She had already dismissed the nymphs as different enough to dislike.

The problem was the wood fairies might think that we were trespassing. Even though the forest didn't belong to one clan, the wood fairies behaved as though it was theirs because of the number of trees.

If they had a problem, they would expose Lionel through some antic or other. "We will see for ourselves tonight. Is it permitted that my apprentice observes them?"

"I do not care. It is their land. We do not go there. You are welcome to walk through any path you need." Her voice was fading, and I assumed she was running away.

"Quinn Larson, what are you doing in the forest? Blind men should stay on an even path."

"Olan, it's been a while." I hadn't seen him since The Morrigan had graciously reversed the spell she'd used to turn him from a pixie to a chickadee. "You have some new neighbors."

"Ah, yes. The lovely synymphs. Delightful creatures."

Lionel must have gotten over his shock, because he said, "Synymphs?" His curiosity rang through the word.

Olan laughed. "Yes, they call themselves that. I suppose they are different enough from our nymphs that they are entitled to a new name. Are you interested in an introduction?"

It figured that Olan had already made himself comfortable with the newcomers. "Not an introduction, but information would be useful," I said. Dirant would probably be the one to do the introduction if we needed one.

"They are interesting enough, but they are still only nymphs. Why do you need information?" Olan asked.

I told him what had happened to the fairies. "So, we thought maybe the scrap of cloth was from one of them."

"I haven't seen them putting anything into a hoard. But then I don't know everything, and they do wander." Olan didn't sound too interested in the problem. It was like he had something more important to think about.

I didn't know what to make of the information. They were chatty, they were standoffish, they were just nymphs. Their wandering seemed to be the only common information. "Do you think they can wander far enough to steal from the fairies?"

"I don't know how far they go to be honest. I can find out when I get back," Olan said.

It would have been nice to have Olan there tonight to keep his eye on Lionel and Dirant. "Where are you going?"

"Oregon," he answered. "I have a cousin there and he is having some problems with the neighbors. I think I can help him."

He would be gone a while, then. "We'll be fine, don't worry. By the time you get back, this will be all finished. Take care of yourself and your cousin."

I had just finished saying goodbye when Lionel grabbed at my arm. "One more visitor." I heard awe in his voice.

A voice rumbled through my ears. It felt like I was hearing him in the marrow of my bones. "I heard what you wanted." It was Moss, the oldest sprite in the city. The last time I saw him, he topped out at about fifteen feet tall. sprites got taller as they aged and gathered more territory. He continued, "These new ones are not who you seek, Quinn. Leave them to settle in."

Even if it was Moss, I couldn't just take his word for it. "Can you tell us why you believe that?"

Lionel squeezed my arm and whispered, "Don't make him mad."

I rolled my eyes at how easy he was to impress. Moss apparently agreed with my interpretation because he chuckled and the ground shook. "I am not so easily angered, young man. I have listened to the others who gave you advice. I do know how far the synymphs roam and it is much farther than others of the nymphkind, but they do not leave the park. They do not speak to the fairies because the fairies do not speak to them. It seems that they do not speak to many people."

I still wanted Lionel to observe the synymphs tonight, if only to learn something about an unfamiliar type of Real Folk. I told

Moss and he agreed. "It is always worth gaining knowledge. They will be safe tonight."

"Thank you, Moss." I felt better knowing Moss might be watching over them. Imps can be like fraternity brothers. They'd party at the drop of a hat and Lionel was more likely to be studying in his room all night than out earning a hangover. Not a good combination.

Moss rumbled, "Give my greeting to Beacon. Tell him that I expect a visit soon." He moved off in a rustle of leaves.

CHAPTER 6

We buried the ashes from the spell and made our way back downtown to the warmth and comfort of Banks'. It was only mid-afternoon, but there was a chill in the air that sucked the warmth from deep inside the marrow of my bones. Winter was visiting and that meant we'd have rain soon. With luck, we'd be finished in the forest before it started.

Inside the bar, it was warm, and smoky, and smelled of stew, and beer, and something that made me feel safe. I couldn't put my finger on what that was, a hit of my mother's perfume? A trace of a lullaby?

"Find me a seat and then you can go back to the park." I waited for Lionel to move me, but he just stood there. "Are you having second thoughts? We can always come back to the synymphs later. If we do, we can both try to find these humans."

"Uh, no. But maybe I should rethink the plan." He stepped closer and took my elbow. "In fact, maybe we should just go home."

I wasn't going home for anything less than an apocalyptic event. "Is someone here?"

"Yes, the twins." He tried to push me back the way we had come. "They haven't seen us yet, but when they do it's not going to be pretty."

"Will they be able to see us?" I half hoped they would because it was no fun being blind, and half hoped they wouldn't because they didn't deserve to be having fun.

"Well, they are playing darts, so I hope so."

He gave me a little push, but I didn't move. "We need to get this over with. Let's confront them," I said. The words carried more optimism than I felt.

Lionel muttered something under his breath that sounded suspiciously like he was calling me an idiot. I chose to ignore it and said, "Don't fret. Mark won't let them fight us here. I want to find out how they're feeling. If only so I can be prepared if they plan to jump us in an alley."

He touched my elbow and I let him lead me to the back of the bar. The dartboard was right next to the door that opened onto an underground passage to the sidhe court.

"Oh, look. It's Quinn Larson. The fairies' pet wizard." I think it was Owen speaking.

"Are we going to have a problem?" I asked.

"I don't know why you would ask that. We are just playing darts," the same twin said.

I couldn't quite get the read I wanted from just his voice; it was too smooth. "Well remember I don't start anything. I just finish things. No matter who starts them."

"You think you've finished it?" The pugnacity came through loud and clear. "We will decide when it's finished."

Before I could respond another sidhe said, "Owen, just let it go. You know what Maeve said."

"Fine, we don't have a problem," Owen snarled.

I wondered what Maeve had said to make him back down so quickly. "Good. Now, Lionel, let's find ourselves a chair." I gave his elbow a little tug. I didn't want to push our luck by staying until Owen found his response.

When Lionel settled me at the table, I sent him on his way. "We'll talk about this in the morning when you get back. I'm fine here. Beacon will be by soon to talk to me."

Lionel was not so confident. "How will you get home? I don't trust those two."

"Don't worry. I'm sure Beacon will walk me home and make sure I'm safely indoors." He was getting a bit annoying with the overprotective act. "I did manage before you came along, you know."

"Yes, but you could see." He tsked and then said, "I know, I know, you'll be fine. I'll see you in the morning."

I heard him clump away and then Mark plonked a beer down in front of me. "I can get someone to sit with you, if you like."

"I'm not helpless. But if Beacon comes in, could you send him over?"

"I will. And I'll keep you supplied with beer."

My stomach growled. "Some stew would be nice. Just put it on my tab. I am going to pay for my drinks, too. It's too tempting to drink for free and that smoke absorbent spell wasn't that hard to put together."

Mark grunted and walked away. I sipped my beer and listened to what was going on around me. Nothing interesting. Mostly gossip, but not about anything I was interested in.

The smell of stew brought my attention back to the table. "Beacon's on his way over," Mark growled after he placed the bowl in front of me.

It took Beacon a while to get to my table. He was social, even for a sprite, and the room sounded full. He sat beside me and tapped my arm. "I have more information."

As much as I wanted to hear it, I needed to pass on a message first. "Good to hear. We ran into Moss earlier. He says he's missing you."

Beacon groaned. "He probably wants to tell me some esoteric piece of sprite law. I swear he thinks he's at the end of his life and this is his last chance to educate the next generations. I'll go see him in a couple of days."

I didn't care when he visited. I just needed to pass on the information. If I didn't, Moss would make sure I got hit by pinecones the next time I was in range. "What have you found out?"

"The rumors were about a group of four humans. They are Goths, apparently. Did you know some humans pretend to be vampires? If they only knew. Anyway, I know where they hang out."

It seemed far too easy that we got a location when just yesterday it was all vague rumors. "Who told you this?"

"I can't tell you, but it is trustworthy information." I snorted. Beacon continued, "No one had asked about it before. This person saw them doing the ritual. And when they heard what happened to Cate, they were scared that someone would blame the kids."

I didn't know what I would have done if I had this information a month ago. Probably got myself killed trying to exact revenge or killed the Goths before asking questions. "I guess we are going to check them out," Beacon said.

"I'm still not convinced this could be humans." I handed my empty glass toward Mark, he'd just thunked a full one on the table. "That's my last. I need to keep my head."

Mark took the empty and said, "Fine. I guess Lionel will appreciate me keeping you this side of blind drunk. Oh sorry, that was insensitive."

I laughed. "I'm not that thin skinned."

Mark chuckled, "Thin skinned. Very funny." He clunked away muttering the words. Trolls may have thick skins, but they still had a sense of humor.

"Even though I trust the source, this is hard to believe,"

Beacon said. "The idea that humans could raise a demon, I mean. Just think how many demons we'd be dodging if they could."

"It gives me nightmares. There will be some other explanation. Tell me where we'll find these humans. I'll bet there's a Real Folk hiding close by." I knew there had to be a good explanation.

After a minute, Beacon said, "I hope it's going to be that easy. We'll take care of it, whoever it is. You and me. No need for Lionel to get involved in the bloody stuff."

I don't know why he wanted to protect Lionel, but I couldn't think of a way to get my apprentice to sit on the sidelines.

I also didn't know how I was going to reconcile my spirit oath with what I really wanted to do to the person who caused Cate's death, but I'd figure something out. "We should get started. Tell me the details."

"It's two boys and two girls. They hang out at this Goth club every night. They will be there in a couple of hours. You want to go look?"

"Yes, but what exactly is a Goth?" If we needed disguises, I would need to get working on the glamours right away.

"Like I said teenagers who act like they are vampires. They dress in black and lacy stuff. They keep their skin pale and they have attitude," Beacon said, with all the impatience of a just-out-of-his-teens sprite.

I rolled my eyes. "Teenagers all have attitude. So how do we get close?"

Beacon cleared his throat. "I can go in with a glamour, can you make my skin look more human? Less barklike? Then I can let you know what I see."

"We could go that way, but I can go in." I fingered the nut that Selencia had given me. "I am worried that the lighting will be wrong, and they'll see through the glamour."

"But how are you going to see?"

I told him about the sight spell. "I think this is as good a reason as anything to use it."

"I should still get a disguise and be there." I could hear reluctance and relief in his voice.

"I can make you look more human, but if there's any kind of black light in the club you can't come in. You know glamours react oddly in that kind of light and it's common in clubs – or it used to be. The last thing we need is for you to look like a mirror or a blur."

He grunted. "Okay. But if we find out who did summon the demon, we lure them somewhere that I can get in on the punishment. Right?"

"Yes. I promise, okay. So, I need to get togged up for the club. Can you walk me home? I can offer you sandwiches and tea."

"One more beer before we leave?" Beacon asked.

"You go ahead. I'm fine. Are the sidhe twins still playing darts?"

"Yes. I heard they were laid up for a day or two. You wouldn't know anything about that, would you?"

I smiled. "Not officially. Is there another sidhe with them?"

"A skinny one, red curly hair like Fionuir's. Why?"

"I got a weird feeling about him. The twins deferred to him earlier and that's not like them. They like to show they don't listen to anyone, but he was able to calm them down. Do you know who he is?"

"I've seen him around, but I don't know his name. Do you want me to find out who he is?" Beacon seemed to have taken on the investigative role very comfortably.

I thought it over for a few minutes, but eventually decided that it wasn't worth sending Beacon after this bit of information. If this sidhe was going to cause trouble, he would do that whether I knew his name or not. "Let's just concentrate on our mysterious humans."

Beacon drained his beer and gave a loud belch. "Right, let's go. I'm curious to see a blind wizard make me a sandwich."

We headed towards the door and I heard, "Bye bye, Quinn. Give my regards to your fairy masters."

I just sighed and shook my head. I don't know if the twins got the contempt I tried to put into the gesture, but since I couldn't see, I could imagine their faces fall in shame and embarrassment. The image made me smile.

CHAPTER 7

Later that afternoon just before four, Beacon and I stood outside a bar. It was on the corner of the block, windows wrapped around the building and you could see most of the inside. I was dressed in a black tee-shirt, tight black jeans, and a black velvet jacket – I felt like an idiot. Beacon looked pretty much as usual; green shirt, brown pants and jacket. The only difference was his skin. Now it looked human, usually it had a brown cast. Not tanned, but tree like, with a light grainy pattern.

"I don't think you can go in." I pointed at the glasses on the bar. "See how they glow?"

He nodded. "I'll hang out on the corner here and watch you. You have about an hour, right?"

My sight had returned a few minutes ago. Beacon had told me when the kids we were waiting for went in, and then I swallowed the seed with Selencia's spell. The world had gradually lightened and come back into focus. It was going to hurt to lose my sight again. Everything was sharp and clear. The colors were richer than I remembered, and I tried to imprint them on my memory for later.

Beacon waited until I nodded and then continued. "The four you want are sitting at the table in the center of the windows. See, the boy with the black hair tied in a ponytail with the red ribbon? That's them."

I looked, two girls and two boys. The other boy had blond spiky hair and was wearing eye liner I could see from here. The two girls were pretty; one had long blond hair, and the other black hair that was so densely dyed it was blue. "I'll have one drink and be back before the spell runs out."

Beacon gave me the thumbs up and moved away to lean against the side of the building. I cast a look-away spell so he would be hard to notice, and then crossed the road.

The bar was better lit than I expected. And because of that, I could watch my four teenagers without having to sit at the next table, and chance that they would suspect I was listening. "Can I get a beer, please?" I asked the bartender.

"We don't do beer, just cocktails for the adults."

Great, a pretentious Goth bar. "I'll have an obituary. You know what that is?"

He nodded, "Gin, vermouth, and absinthe."

He placed a martini glass on the bar and reached for the two bottles on the glass shelves. He held them high and free poured, then flipped the bottles before putting them back on the shelf. I tossed a twenty on the bar and sipped the drink. It was good, so I nodded my approval.

Then I turned to look at the table of teenagers. They looked normal for human teenagers. I couldn't hear what they were saying, but the table behind them was empty. I kept my eyes on the four as I made my way to the seat, but I slipped into my Real Sight.

Instead of seeing a glamour, I saw nothing. I stood frozen for a second, then reached out tentatively for a chair that I remembered was just to my right. I had to act normal. Not an easy task when every nerve in my body was screaming at me to run. As I turned the chair so I could sit, the room flashed back into focus. I placed my glass on the table and sat. My Real Sight was working and the panic receded.

The two boys and the black-haired girl didn't change with my Real Sight. The blonde girl did. She had a glamour on her. It was an elegant construction. There was a faint shimmer at the edge of her body, as though she was outlined in mother-of-pearl, but that was the only indication. I couldn't see if it changed her appearance completely, or whether it simply enhanced what she had.

No matter what the glamour did, she must have some contact with the Real Folk. There was no other way to get a glamour.

I quickly cast a spell to look through the disguise, but it just bounced off. The girl rolled her shoulders when I did it. Add the fact she felt my casting to the list of not right things about her.

Sitting next to them, I was careful to not seem too interested – no need to come across as the creepy guy. I let their chatter roll past me without showing I was listening. I took a sip of my drink and nothing happened to my sight. I guess making the shift from one to the other took some power from the spell.

"Can you get away from the parents? If we could all go to the concert it would be so perfect." This from the dark-haired girl.

"I can; no prob. My folks are out of town. Jase here can tell his parents he's staying at mine." The shorter boy answered.

This was not giving me anything I could use. I had to leave in about fifteen more minutes. For the next ten minutes, they kept planning how to trick their parents so they could go to this concert. The blonde-haired girl didn't contribute much to the conversation. Now that I was closer, I could see worry in her blue eyes.

The dark-haired boy, Jase, turned to her. "Dionne, can you get away?"

She played with the straw in her glass. "The foster parents

don't care what I do. I'll be fine." Her words came out with all the world-weariness of a teenager trying to sound unconcerned.

"What is wrong with you?" The black-haired girl whined. "You've been like this since we did that stupid ceremony."

"Sorry," Dionne said. "I know it's stupid, but something happened that night. I felt something happen."

"Oh god, not again." The blond boy threw his head back theatrically. "Nothing happened. It was a total bust. I don't know if we didn't do it right, or if it was bullshit. But nothing happened."

"Fine," Dionne said, apparently tired of the argument.

My sight started to get blurry then, so I tossed back the last of my obituary and headed back to where Beacon was waiting.

"YOU WANT TO GO HOME?" BEACON ASKED WHEN I WAS WITHIN earshot. "Or we can get a coffee and talk."

With the last of my fading sight I glanced in the window of the coffee house then looked back across the street. "You'll be able to see what's going on if we have coffee. We can always get a cab home."

I kept a few hundred dollars on me at all times. Real Folk worked on bargaining and most survived off the land. And really most wouldn't pass as humans, so they didn't need money. I tossed a few bills on the table. I kept looking as my vision faded; the bright sunshine, the deep green of the rhododendron bushes, the flash of cars— red, silver, and finally black. I was back at day one. I missed knowing what people were doing around me. I missed being able to read the reaction in their expressions. I missed...shit I just missed light.

Beacon put the mug of coffee in my hand and I heard his chair scrape as he repositioned it. "Quinn?" his voice broke through my wallowing. "Are you okay? You look like you are going to cry. Don't do it, I don't think humans cry in public."

"I'm fine. I was just feeling sorry for myself, poor little blind wizard."

Beacon touched my arm. "I'm sure you will find a cure soon."

At least he was confident. I couldn't raise the same feeling. Now that it was time to tell him what I had learned, I was having some difficulty putting it into words. "They were nervous about something. That radiated off them even though they only talked about teenage stuff."

"So, just tell me. Maybe you'll figure it out by talking."

"Well before I forget, here's what I saw. Of the four of them, the blonde is the one with more than just concerts and dress-up to her. The others are just humans. She's got someone keeping a glamour on her." I didn't tell him about the momentary loss of sight because it wasn't important to what I had learned.

"What does she really look like? Maybe she's got some kind of disfigurement. Maybe someone is doing her a favor?"

That would be unusual enough, but not impossible. Sometimes fairies took pity on humans and you never knew why. "She is in a foster home. Maybe there was someone living near where she was born."

"It's possible," Beacon said. "But what was under the glamour?"

"That's another weird thing. To me she looked the same under the glamour. I think it's been there a long time. Have you ever heard of someone who spent, what, about sixteen years under a glamour?"

Beacon didn't answer right away. He was older than me so had more memories to sift. "No. Glamours are only used for a couple of days at the longest. Most of them for only a couple of hours. You think she's grown into it? That would be something, hey?"

If the humans thought they could model their kids from birth, they'd be all over it. "I'll get Lionel to research it."

"They are leaving, you want to follow them?"

I thought about it for all of ten seconds. "No. I can't see, so I don't know what we would learn. There's plenty of other ways to find out where she lives. Let's go home."

We didn't talk in the taxi. It's not a good idea to chat in human presence. You never know how they will interpret what they hear.

Beacon walked me to the front door and got me inside. "I've been thinking. Maybe you couldn't see what was beneath the glamour because you didn't have full sight."

"Crap, you don't think Selencia pulled a fast one? I guess I was so desperate to see that I didn't even think about the fact she might put a bit of deviltry into the spell." So maybe the glitch in the bar was just a trick.

Beacon sighed. "Well, you know fairies."

Then I realized that if she had only given me single sight, like humans, I wouldn't have seen the glamour. Still, there could be a limit to what it would do. "Maybe we should have Lionel check her out. If he sees through the glamour, we'll know Selencia pulled a trick, and if not, we'll at least know where to start researching."

"Good idea. Where is Lionel anyway?"

"He's checking out something in the park. I don't expect him back until early morning." I realized this was the first time since I went blind that I had been alone. "Can I get you a sandwich or something?" I hoped he would say no, but I had to offer.

"No, I'm ready for bed. Do you want me to stay until Lionel gets back?"

It was time for me to try to manage a bit on my own. It was suddenly annoying me that I'd let myself become so dependent. "I might as well start learning how to get along. I'll be fine."

Beacon clapped me on the shoulder. "Good luck. I'll come back for breakfast."

Alone, I started feeling my way around the main floor of my house, forming a mental map of the furniture. I reached into my imagination to place *my* couch there, not just *a* couch. It seemed to help. I stopped grasping at furniture after a few passes, realizing I wasn't going to fall over something.

I'd pass on dinner. It was probably best for me to have someone supervise when I cooked the first time.

CHAPTER 8

I woke early, and the house was silent. As I was making my way around the house last night, I realized that I didn't need to see, just remember. After that it got a lot easier. I'd made myself walk from my couch to my bed without reaching out to check for wandering furniture. I barked my hip on the kitchen counter, but other than that I was proud that I made it.

"Outside is going to be a much bigger challenge," I reminded myself. I was used to waking to the smell of coffee, and this morning there was nothing. Maybe I could surprise Lionel with a pot of freshly brewed beans.

I felt through my closet and found jeans and a tee-shirt. At least I'd been dressing myself all along. I took a minute to visualize the kitchen. I hoped Lionel hadn't done too much reorganizing.

I managed to find the coffee, fill the pot, and get it going. My stomach growled so I felt around until I found bread. Unfortunately, it was unsliced. I got a bit queasy thinking of the damage I could do feeling my way through slicing bread and decided to have an apple.

It wasn't long before the house smelled like fresh coffee. I drank mine black to avoid having to deal with milk. It was a bit strong but drinkable.

Lionel hadn't stirred yet, so I went over and knocked on his door. No answer. This was starting to worry me, he never slept in. I hated to violate his privacy, but I needed to know he was all right. I turned the handle and gave the door a push. "Lionel?" I kept my voice low. If he was sleeping, I didn't want to shock him awake – that was never a good idea with a wizard.

Still no sound. I should have been able to hear him breathing. I made my way to the bed and ran my hand along the bottom of the sheets. They were cold. Lionel hadn't made it home.

I went back to the kitchen, much less hesitant than earlier. I refilled my coffee cup and started thinking about how I could find Lionel with spells. Spells I would be able to do without causing too much of a problem if I got them wrong.

A summoning wouldn't work. A spirit wouldn't do as much damage as a demon, but if I let one out there would be repercussions. I didn't want to deal with cleaning up after a spirit had celebrated a moment of freedom in my home. And I couldn't figure out how I could be sure the casting circle was closed without being able to see it.

I had a few seeker stones. It meant going down into the workshop alone, but if I was careful, I wouldn't fall and break anything. I knew where the stones were. I would be able to tell by feeling which ones were auditory. "Okay, down we go."

I pulled open the door and gingerly made my way down the stairs. I lost track and jarred my leg by trying go down one step too many. But that was better than one too few.

The stones were in a bowl on the far side of the worktable. I took a second to visualize the room. If I fell into the center pit, I'd break something and then I'd have to wait for someone to find me. I hugged the table as I walked, not sure how much room was between the edge of the table and the side of the pit. Knowing I had never come close to falling in didn't help. It was too easy to get disoriented when you couldn't see.

I managed to avoid knocking over any of the bottles that my fingers brushed. And the bowl was right at the end where I'd expected it to be.

I picked at the stones and sorted out one that felt like the bowl of a spoon. I warmed it between my fingers to activate it and heard a hum start to rise. I raised Dirant's image in my mind, and then whispered his name. The humming rose and dipped for a few seconds, and then the wood imp's voice came from the stone.

"I was sleeping. What do you want?"

"It's Quinn."

"So? Big deal, I was still sleeping. What do you want at this hour? It's barely sunrise."

"I seem to be one apprentice short this morning. Did you meet Lionel last night?"

"Yes." I heard a groan. "And I have a hangover to prove it. We watched the synymphs for a couple of hours and then came back here to drink some of my special brew."

"Is Lionel there recovering?"

A laugh ground out through the stone. "No. It seems that he is large enough to manage far more than me. It was probably foolish to try to keep up."

I grinned. Imps found it difficult to ignore a challenge, even one that only existed in their own minds. "When did you last see him?"

"It was an hour past midnight. What time is it now?"

"Almost seven. He should be back by now."

"I didn't lose him," Dirant was quick to say.

"No, you are not responsible. Go back to sleep."

I would have to find someone to help me search in person.

Dirant burped and said, "I'll see if I can find anything out for you. If I do, I'll send someone to tell you."

"Thanks," I said and then dropped the stone back in the bowl.

I made it back to the kitchen when I heard the door open. "Lionel?"

"No. Is he not home then?" Beacon called back. He closed the door loudly, not quite a slam, but not far off. Then he joined me in the kitchen. I poured him the last of the coffee as I told him about Lionel.

"Maybe he ran into a lady friend and will be home soon." Beacon chuckled; I'm sure thinking of his own wild oat sowing days. "He's of that age."

I wished that was a possibility. It would help me to stop the series of scenarios running in my head, all versions of Lionel coming to a violent and final end. "I don't think he has any lady friends." My stomach growled. "Have you had breakfast?"

"No, shall we go out? We could look for Lionel on the way to Banks'."

I shook my head. "I want to be here when he gets home. And I'm trying to be more self-sufficient. Why don't you help me make breakfast?"

"Are you sure?" Beacon sounded reluctant.

I laughed at his hesitation. "Are you afraid of blind wizards around open flame? Don't worry; I'm not planning on anything complicated. How about toast? You can make sure I'm not about to slice off a finger. Or oatmeal, I can stir a pot."

"I'm hungry enough for both. How about I make some toast and watch that you don't scorch the oatmeal? You can make enough to last a few days."

And there would be plenty left over if Lionel showed up. We gathered up the ingredients and I started the pot boiling. I put some dried fruit in to soften while Beacon made a fresh pot of coffee.

I found the oatmeal and other ingredients, and then Beacon touched my elbow for attention. He put my hand on the loaf with my fingers touching the cut edge. "Now draw your fingers back and bend the tips under so you form a barrier with your hand. Now carefully guide the knife into the bread using your bent fingers as a gauge."

I sawed slowly and managed two thickish slices. The concentration took my mind off Lionel. Beacon took the slices to toast.

"Do you think you could ask around to see if anyone has seen Lionel, while I wait here?" I asked as I stirred the pot. I could feel the oatmeal thicken against the spoon.

Beacon scraped butter on the toast and my mouth watered with the aroma. I took the oatmeal off the burner to let it rest and finish cooking on the counter.

"Well, you managed to get food ready without burning the house down." Beacon put my hand on the plate. "Eat and we'll figure out what to do about your errant apprentice."

We ate in silence. The scenarios started playing again and I tried to focus my thoughts. It didn't work. Then I tried to decide what I wanted to do between being here to give Lionel a piece of my mind when he returned and going out to search for him.

"Relax, Quinn. He's not a child. You don't need to worry about him."

"What?"

"It's written all over your face. You might want to practice schooling your expression." He slapped my arm in what I'm sure he meant as a friendly pat. I dropped my spoon. "What do you want to do?"

"I'll go mad just sitting here. I can give him a lecture when we find him. Let's go look." I felt for the empty dishes and took them to the sink. "We'll run into humans at this time of day. Let me refresh your glamour."

I cast the spell on Beacon, and he pronounced it successful. "You know, Quinn, that girl? I've been wondering how the glamour lasts through the night? I mean they usually fade when you sleep, right?"

"Yes. I was thinking about that since I got home. She seems

completely unaware of the glamour, so I'm guessing this has been going on since she was a baby. There's definitely someone keeping the spell going. It's possible to cast the glamour on an object the person carries, but it's dangerous. If they lose the item, the glamour falls away."

"You'll figure it out." Beacon took my elbow. "Don't worry. We can always find her again and Lionel will help you see what the real cause is."

I liked his confidence, but I was worried about losing the little connection the girl had to Cate's death. If not her – and I refused to believe a human could raise a demon – then whoever protected her, was going to learn what it was like to take love away from a wizard. I swallowed the rising fury. Beacon didn't need to know how much I wanted revenge. "Okay, let's head down to the park. Maybe Dirant has some information now he's had time to recover from the party."

IT WAS ONLY A FIVE-MINUTE WALK. ALONG THE WAY, A FEW humans passed us. Most offered a good morning, none freaked out. So, I guessed my glamour on Beacon really worked.

"Let's head toward Dirant's territory," I said. "We should be able to find some fairies or pixies on the way. If Lionel came through, someone will have seen him."

With Beacon steering me, we made it around to the other side of the lagoon without problems. Even though we were passing through a lot of Real Folk territory most of the inhabitants were sleeping, so we didn't have to stop to chat. We came to a clearing and Beacon asked me to wait. "I should probably see Moss while we're here. I'll be back in ten minutes. He'll understand we're on a mission and won't keep me long."

I nodded. With any luck Dirant or someone would drop by and give me some advice while I waited. I needed to make headway on something soon. Of course, a thousand wood imps could march through the clearing and I wouldn't be the wiser if they wanted to pass unnoticed.

The sounds of the forest filtered back when I was alone. There was the chatter of birds calling and shaking bits of tree to the ground. I heard some tiny animal scrabble through the carpet of leaves. A buzz of insects swooped past my left ear. It was sleep-inducing and I was drifting off when I heard my name.

"Quinn Larson, imagine running into you here." The voice was familiar but I couldn't place it exactly.

"I don't know; a wizard in the forest isn't that unusual. A sidhe getting his shoes dirty is pretty rare though."

"Amusing, but then, you do like to use humor as a weapon; perhaps because you don't have others."

It wasn't one of the twins, but I knew I'd heard that voice recently. Whoever it was, they were making an attempt to disguise their voice. It wasn't a great job, but every time I almost identified him, it slipped away.

I didn't react to his taunt. "Is there something I can do for you?"

"No, but perhaps I can give you some information. I understand you misplaced your apprentice."

Oh, great. What had Lionel gotten himself into now? I placed the voice. It was the sidhe who had calmed the twins down in Banks'. A sidhe I definitely didn't know. And since he hung out with the twins, one I didn't trust. "The last time we met, Owen couldn't be bothered to introduce us. Perhaps you would like to remedy that?"

"Ailin is my name. I already know who you are. Quinn Larson, the wizard who captured Queen Fionuir." His voice hissed with menace.

I heard a soft footfall and shifted my weight slightly, ready to defend myself if he was going to exact vengeance for Fionuir. I couldn't sense anyone with him, but it wouldn't be the first time I missed something I should have caught. "Pleased to meet you, Ailin. You have news of my apprentice?"

A silky chuckle gave me his new location. "He has spent the evening telling us all about you."

I relaxed a bit. If he was going to lie so stupidly, I might not have to fight him. "And what did he tell you?"

"Oh, it's not really important what he told us. It's far more interesting that he has agreed to work with us. I suggest you pack up all his belongings so he can move into the guest quarters."

I couldn't imagine what Ailin was hoping to gain by this. If he wanted to attack, he didn't need to play this stupid game. If he thought I would kick Lionel out, then he needed a better story. Then again, maybe Maeve would be upset to find that her favorite wizard was beaten up by one of her subjects. "If he wants to join you, he just has to say so. Send him home and we can pack him up in about ten minutes."

"Oh, he'll be home soon."

I cast my senses around the clearing. There was definitely only the two of us. Beacon would be back in a few minutes. If Ailin was playing games, he'd have to stop then. "Then I think we are done."

I felt him lean in, his breath in my ear as he spoke, that scent of clove now only a hint of spice. "Oh, we are far from done, wizard. But I'll leave you here."

Then his presence was gone from the clearing. Sidhe can be very weird when they were excited. This one was a major drama queen, but there would be something behind what he was saying. The twins and their new friend were up to some kind of trouble.

Someone started kicking up leaves and snapping dry branches. I started to prepare myself for attack when Beacon called out, "Hey, I didn't want to sneak up on you."

I told him what had just happened.

"Oh, they are up to something all right. Moss says there have been sidhe wandering the forest for the last few weeks. My guess is they are trying to get you and Lionel distrusting each other. If they can drive a wedge between you, they figure they'll crack one of you. I wouldn't be surprised to find they've been whispering in Lionel's ear. But Lionel would not go with them voluntarily."

"Are you sure they are not telling the truth?" It was Dirant. "The lad is missing after all."

I reminded myself that Dirant didn't know Lionel. And from his perspective it was a reasonable question. It was none of his business, but a reasonable question. "I am sure. And unless you have a very good reason for me to change my mind, the conversation is over."

He whined and then said, "I saw a sidhe leave about the same time Lionel did. Maybe he was watching us? Maybe he was waiting for him?"

There were too many maybes for me to change my mind. "Not a chance. If the sidhe have Lionel, he's a prisoner. But I think he can take care of himself."

"Okay, just asking," Dirant said. "I've talked to people and no one saw Lionel after he left here. I remember he was heading across the park, which is where you live, right?"

I nodded.

"Sorry, that's all I got."

"Thanks anyway, Dirant. How's the hangover?"

"He's already gone, Quinn," Beacon said. "Where next?"

I didn't think Lionel was at Banks' and we couldn't just keep walking the city. I didn't really believe he was a captive, but if we had to rescue him from sidhe or anyone else, I'd need to pack some charms and Beacon would need to be ready to back me up.

"Let's go home. You can help me set up a circle and I'll ask some of the spirits I know. And maybe Melbe will be able to check the sidhe court for signs of Lionel; just in case they've taken him prisoner."

As we walked, Beacon hummed to the trees. As a sprite, he was responsible for the health of the forest. Most sprites stayed within the trees, but Beacon had always mixed with the other Real Folk. His song faded as I felt the path turn from dirt to paving. "That should hold me for a week. I just got a lecture from Moss about doing my duty to the forest."

"Don't you live here?" I was curious and figured he would either tell me or say it's none of my business.

"I do, but I spend a lot of time outside because I think we need to know what is going on. I believe that everything that happens outside the trees affects the health of the forest. Not everyone agrees."

I had no idea that there was a division like that in the sprite world. Maybe I was getting too insular for my own good. "It can be hard to convince people to change."

Beacon replied, "They will change, or they won't. I don't try to convince them. I just do what I know is right."

I nodded. "Do you have any ideas about why Ailin was there?"

"I think you might be better waiting for Lionel to show up, in case he saw them last night." Beacon turned into my front garden. "I think he was just trying to drive a wedge like I said. But there is always more than one reason a sidhe does anything."

"True. They are clearly trying to get Fionuir back. If she does get out of the dimensional fold, then she has fifty years to build up support to take back the crown." I almost felt sorry for Maeve. It must be much easier to be queen with no real opponent.

"And trying to punish you for sending her away in the first place," Beacon said before leaving me in my chair. He started to make tea before continuing, "Maybe that was what Ailin was doing? Testing to see how you could be punished. Seeing if you could be pushed into doing something stupid."

"I don't know. Let's leave it for now. My priority is to locate my apprentice. Then I can get back to the human girl and the crazy sidhe— and the fairies." I took Beacon down to the work-room and we started to build the circle and get some information.

After an hour, I'd exhausted my connections and the only

thing I'd learned was that Lionel had been nowhere near the sidhe court.

"I guess we'll head to Banks' and see who's there. When he gets home, unless he has a really great reason for being lost, he's going to be memorizing the lineage of every wizard from Merlin on down."

CHAPTER 9

We were just settling down to a snack, when the door opened with a bang making me spill hot tea all down the front of my shirt. "Lionel, if that's you, we are going to have a long talk about how you should behave."

"I am not your apprentice." Great. Princess was back. "I wish to enter, why have you blocked me?"

"Beacon, can you see if she's alone?"

I felt him move away, and then he said, "It's just her."

"I apologize, Princess. Please come in this one time." I would happily apologize every time she tried to come in, but there was no way I was giving her free run of my home. Since the last time, when she just walked in, and I'd ended up with another fairy problem to solve, I'd removed her permissions and made Lionel check to see if she'd left anything behind that would override the protections.

"You are getting absent minded, wizard," she said as she approached. I imagined her striding down the hall ready to fight if she needed to. "I see you have not yet trained the apprentice to grow flowers in your home. How do you manage to live without growing things around?"

I opened my mouth to argue, but she cut me off. "I have come to hear you explain why you have not yet returned our babies and treasure."

I heard Beacon shift in his seat. He needn't have worried; it looked like she only wanted to harass me.

I tried to get my thoughts in order. "We are investigating some leads, Princess. We have to find out who is taking the treasure before we can attempt to stop them and make them return what they took."

"Princess," Beacon said. "You have dropped something. I would hate to think you would lose other items."

"Oh," I could hear the annoyance in her voice. "Yes, I must take more care."

Sneaky little fairy, thinking I wouldn't be able to see her put five things in my home so she could avoid the permissions.

"What are you doing to find this culprit? Perhaps I can get you some help." She'd dropped the imperial tone.

"Lionel is currently researching a lead," I said. It would be helpful to have the fairies snooping, but they were not the most reliable informants. And if they had information, they would have found the culprit and I wouldn't be here. Although maybe they knew something they didn't realize was important. "It would be of assistance if the fairies could pass on any hints they might overhear." I regretted the words as they came out. I'd have fairies dropping by at all hours, passing on gossip that would waste my time.

"Of course, I'll speak to the clan leaders," Princess said.

Beacon moved beside me and I felt him bend and straighten. I had no idea what he was trying to convey.

"We will be out investigating. Perhaps the best way to pass on information is to arrange a drop off point." Some place that I could have Lionel check.

"Yes, we can leave the messages with Mark at Banks',"

Princess announced. "Be sure you start checking them tonight. I will leave you to your work."

Beacon chuckled and I felt him move again. "One moment, Princess, you have forgotten these."

I heard her displeasure as she stomped out of the house. Fairies could make all kinds of noise if they wanted. The door closed and Beacon came back. "She was dropping little beads all the time. It's like she thought I would stop noticing."

"I can't believe she's trying to pull something like that when I'm helping her. Then again, she's a fairy. She's bound to think of some spell she can cast to hide her behavior next time. I'll have to make sure we meet outside."

"I'm not sure even that will work. Maybe Lionel can find a spell that will repel fairies so they can only meet you somewhere else."

I stopped worrying about fairies invading my home and returned to worrying about my apprentice. I hadn't wanted one in the first place, but now I was used to Lionel. And, I got a kick out of teaching someone. "Maybe I should have asked Princess to have the fairies look for Lionel."

Beacon poured more tea. "If you had, she'd still be here, and I'd have missed enough of her damn beads to allow her access. Don't fret. He's not a kid. He'll be okay, or he'll find a way to contact you."

Intellectually I believed that. In reality, with The Morrigan flying around touching people – usually meaning death or disfigurement— and some crazy sidhe trying to threaten me, my gut said it was highly likely he was in a major pile of trouble.

CHAPTER 10

Beacon headed down to Banks' to let Mark know about his impending fairy message drop role and see if anyone had any news that would help us. I spent some time going through the contents of my kitchen cupboards. Practicing identifying things by feel and making a mental shopping list.

Despite the mundane task, I felt some burden drop away from me with every item I picked up. A burden I hadn't realized was there. Cate's death was horrible. My stomach clenched with the memory of finding her slumped against that doorway. Any time I let the memory through, it was as fresh as if it had just happened. When I realized she was dead, the light had gone out of my life. Losing my sight, only days later, just made it official.

I guess deciding to put Cate's death behind me was just the first step. Trying to become independent was doing more to heal me than just will power.

The door opened and I felt the chill of the afternoon breeze. I waited, fingering a net spell in my pocket. If Princess had left things behind, she was going to find out what it meant to try to trick a wizard.

"Oh, there you are," Lionel said. "I'm sorry I was – what are you doing?"

I let go of the spell. "Never mind what I'm doing. Where the hell have you been?"

Lionel touched my hand. He liked to let me know when he was near ever since he'd startled me when I was forming bee-balls. His fingers were like ice.

"I was on my way out of the park when three druids stopped me." There was awe in his voice. "I've never talked to even one druid. They are so reclusive; I'd wondered if they were just legends."

"Reclusive is one way to put it." I carefully placed the kettle on the stove and lit the gas. "Detached from the world in such a way as to seem uncaring about what is going on, is another way."

"You're making tea." I couldn't tell if he was impressed or worried.

"Yep, you've been gone long enough that I needed to learn a few skills." I remembered his worry that I wouldn't need him and would kick him out. "Don't fret. I would much rather have you do this. I only get one chance to screw up and blow the house to smithereens."

He laughed and gave me a gentle push to the counter. "Then let me do it." The worry had dropped from his voice and I was listening to an older, wiser Lionel.

"I guess you had better tell me all about your time with the druids."

Lionel made a sound of agreement. "First I should tell you what we saw the synymphs doing. It wasn't much. I think they are just settling in. You know, finding their way around the neighborhood." The dry tinkle of leaves hitting the teapot punctuated his words. "They are definitely wearing shoes made of that material. But I don't think they have the ability to get as far as Banks'."

"What makes you think that?" I didn't want to get on the

wrong track because of an assumption. "We found the scrap of material there."

"When I was leaving, I saw one of them, the smaller female. It was like she hit a kind of wall. She was wandering and looking at everything, and suddenly she got all pale and came to a complete stop. She was swaying, like she was going to pass out. I was so worried I almost went to help her. Then she turned around and went back the way she'd come. After a few steps, she gained her color back."

Interesting. "Maybe they can extend their range over time."

Lionel poured water into the pot before speaking. "Even if you're right, they have a long way to go to get as far as Banks'. That's if they can manage on the city streets. I didn't see them even venture onto the packed earth paths while we watched."

I wasn't ready to cross off the synymphs from the cast of characters involved in the theft, but I could accept that maybe someone was setting them up.

Lionel continued speaking after a minute. "It's odd that Dirant didn't tell you this. He said he'd contact you this morning."

"Well, he was a little hung-over this morning. I should have probably asked more questions, but I was more interested in any information he had on you."

"Sorry, I thought I was only with the druids for a few hours."

"Never mind, tell me what happened there."

He slurped at his tea. "Is there any bread? I haven't eaten since dinner."

If I got a chance to talk to a druid, I'd give them some clear instructions on the care and feeding of apprentices; perhaps punctuated with my staff on their heads. "I made oatmeal. I can heat that up for you." I heard him push back his chair and waved him down. "No. I need the practice. You won't always be here to help. And even while you are here, you need to get out more."

I used some of the hot water from the kettle to soften the

leftover oatmeal and squeezed some honey on top. "Here, it's warm and filling."

"Um, is there more without the ketchup?"

I laughed. "Not honey, then? Maybe we need a labeling method before I make everything inedible."

He got himself a new serving and for a few minutes all I heard was the spoon against the bowl.

When he was done, he said, "Thanks, that was great. And maybe there's a market for savory oatmeal."

"Funny. So, tell me about the druids." I resolved to keep my questions to a minimum, giving him full reign to tell his story.

"They took me to the museum. It's so cool inside. When the druids are there, the exhibits seem to come to life. I saw battles waging in the pictures. You know the sword they have under the water? It glows, there are words on it. History lives at the museum."

I bit my lips to cut off my comment that he might want to study there instead of with me. I didn't like the feeling I got with the idea of him gone.

"Sorry. Anyway, they asked me what I knew about the Gur amulet. Apparently, they just noticed it was missing."

"I will never understand druid priorities. It was full of the souls of murdered druids; how could they forget about it?"

"I asked about that. They said as long as the souls sleep, they are fine, but recently they heard some signs that the stone was awakening."

Oh, that was not good news. "How recently?"

"They were pretty vague about that. I get the feeling that time is different for them."

We had discussed giving the amulet back to the druids after we cleansed it, but I didn't want them having it if they weren't going to take care of it. If someone got their hands on such a powerful battery again, it would be disastrous. But I knew that was wrong, it wasn't my responsibility. "I guess we should give it back. It's going to take a while to retrieve it."

"I can get the spell ingredients together. Who will we send to bring it?" Lionel asked.

The amulet was hidden in Tierra del Fuego at the bottom of a lake. We'd sent it in a relay of Real Folk all the way down in four days. "We could invite one of the wizards from there to come for a visit and bring the amulet with him. If we give him a pass code, he can transport himself in a matter of hours," I said.

"Do you really want a strange wizard here?"

Lionel was right. Once a stranger was here, it would take a lot of power to send him back. And I needed to concentrate on my current problems. "What about asking Moss to help? He has connections with every type of sprite on this side of the world. And probably on a few other continents too," I said.

Lionel couldn't see any problem with that idea, at least as an idea. "But maybe Beacon should ask," he suggested. "I don't know about you, but Moss kind of scares me. He's likely to ask for something in exchange that will take a long time to fulfill."

"I don't know if he's that scary, but we'll ask Beacon," I said.

A HALF HOUR LATER, I WAS LISTENING TO LIONEL READ OUT the descriptions of summoning spells we found in my books. I worried that I'd forgotten something that would retrieve other people's property.

So far, no luck in the six books we'd studied. I could develop a spell, but that took three things I didn't have in supply right now: time, energy, and patience to experiment.

"It might be better if we had a spell though, so we could just summon the Gur amulet. Then we wouldn't take the chance of being beholden to Moss," Lionel said.

He seemed to think Moss was some sort of sprite godfather. I did think about summoning the amulet, but there were limitations. "The problem with a summoning is obstructions. I shudder to imagine the damage an amulet made of stone would do as it rushed through the distance between the southernmost tip of South America to here."

"So how is that different from summoning the fairy treasure and babies?" Lionel asked. "If they have to travel then they will pass through human territory. Hard to explain flying treasure, let alone tiny fairy babies."

"Good point. I'm impressed that you're learning to think things through." He was getting there, but he'd missed one component of the spell we were looking for. "So, tell me again what we want in a spell."

"Well most of the spells we've found contain an element of locating and returning. The problem we've got is that when it's your own stuff you are trying to find, you have a solid description."

I nodded.

"So, in order to find something that doesn't belong to you, you have to use other identifiers. We don't have enough information to describe the fairy treasure that is missing, to locate it."

I waited, but he seemed to have run out of ideas. I prompted, "If we can find a spell that summons other people's stuff, we'll find the locater part of the spell. Summoning is pretty straight forward. You want it to come or you want it brought. If we do that..."

I heard him draw in a breath. "Okay, I get it. If we have the locater part, we can craft a spell to locate anything. If we need it brought, we can add that part. Hey, could we modify it to locate the reason that girl is living under a glamour."

When I'd brought Lionel up to date on the teenagers, he'd made notes but had no suggestions. I'd hoped something he'd learned from Cate would help us, but now his creativity was more valuable than information.

"I'll have to give that some thought," I was intrigued by the idea. It hadn't occurred to me to use the spell for information. "It will be a different spell, I think. But a good idea. I'm impressed."

"Quinn, are you down there?" Beacon couldn't even open the door to my workshop without my presence. Even Lionel couldn't get at most of the contents of the room, but he could come down and look through most of the books.

"We'll be up in a second." I told Lionel to put the books we'd already reviewed back on the shelf and felt my way to the stairs.

"We might have a problem," Beacon sounded more amused than alarmed.

"Mark doesn't want to take the messages?" I guessed.

"Oh, no that's fine with him. But by the time I got there he had already received more than a hundred notes."

"What notes?" Lionel asked.

I told him about Princess and he laughed. "So, we are going to be inundated with fairy gossip. Don't worry I'll go through them. I can read fast."

I was tempted to say, 'ignore them', but there would probably be something we could use. "I think we need to re-prioritize. We have too many things on the go: the fairy problem, the Gur amulet, and the teenage demon summoning."

"What's this about the amulet? I thought it was safe," Beacon asked, reminding me that he needed to be brought up to date.

Lionel told Beacon about the druids while I tried to make sense of all the demands on my time.

"You really need to deal with the druids," Beacon said. "They have a long history of punishing people who don't cooperate. You know they can block your powers."

"I know but if I don't deal with the fairies, I'll be driven crazy by their clues." I figured Princess would keep ramping up the nagging until the treasure was back.

It was as good an opportunity as any to ask him to talk to his grandfather. I told him what the plan was for retrieving the amulet. "So, if he agrees, we can concentrate on the rest of the list until the druids come calling, or until we can give them the amulet."

"Sure, I think the old guy is kind of afraid of the druids too. Don't tell him I said that. But I think you left out one important item on your list. You need to figure out if the Gur druids awakening had anything to do with you."

My stomach twisted at the thought I'd had anything to do with rousing the souls of murdered druids. "Oh, gods I hope not. Right now, I'm favoring the plan to ignore that. At least until we make some progress on the other two problems."

Beacon left us after giving Lionel a bag that, by the sound of it, was filled with the scraps of paper and dry bark that fairies used to write notes on.

Lionel sighed. "This is going to take some time."

"Yes. I guess our priorities have been set for us. We'll get the fairies dealt with first, and then go back to the teenagers. I hope they don't find a way to cause more damage in the meantime – if it was them in the first place."

And we'll pretend we don't have a looming problem with the druids. That made me realize I was also a little afraid of them. I told myself it was just fear of the unknown. My gut said, 'think again.'

We took lunch down to the workshop after I cast stronger protections on my doors and windows. I had a nagging feeling we were due for some kind of intrusion. Only a few specific people would be able to get through any of the openings to my home without an invitation.

There were six books left to peruse for a versatile seeking spell, so it took less than an hour to come to the end. If such a spell existed, and I can't believe there wasn't one, I didn't have a copy.

"Is there any chance we won't have to create a spell?" Lionel sounded like he hoped the answer was no. I couldn't blame him, creating a new spell was a rite of graduation for an apprentice. Usually they just created a simple one though.

"No, but we'll build it in steps. I promise, you will learn how to craft a new spell, but I need to know you won't try anything until I say you are ready."

"Okay," he sulked out the word.

"I need your oath. Even in the best of circumstances, things will go wrong when you do it the first time. These aren't the best of circumstances."

He sighed again; apparently, the maturity he developed in the druid's presence was fading. "I swear on my powers that I will not experiment with new spells until you deem me ready."

Thankfully, the words, not the attitude, made the difference. I knew he'd push the boundaries on the oath, but he couldn't make a completely new spell without permission – and my permission would come when I could see what he was up to. "Let's use those notes to test your spell craft. Help me down into the pit. We'll draw a circle and you can empty the bag in the center."

When we were seated, I heard a shiver of sound that must have represented more than the couple of hundred notes Beacon had mentioned.

"Okay, I can sort them into some order if you like," Lionel offered.

"No, that's the first step in the spell. We'll test some logic on sorting. If we can figure out how to get the dross out of the pile, we can figure out how to sort missing fairy treasure from the stores they have left."

He sighed. "I should have thought of that."

"No, you shouldn't have. You forget sometimes how little time you have had to learn. I'm going to start relying on you less for the day to day and focus more on teaching. We'll start right now. What else might be important about the idea of sorting notes about missing items from similar ones?"

Lionel made a humming sound that I'd come to realize was his way of focusing his thinking. I needed to add to the curriculum a way to do that silently. "Do you think the thief thought of that? Maybe they leave a little behind to confuse a seeking spell."

"Yes. I'm pretty sure they did think of it." Now I had him in learning mode, I continued, "Think about three ways we can ask to sort the pile of messages so we lose the gossip and keep anything that might help."

"Help in getting the treasure or help in any of the problems?"

Damn, when he concentrated he was sharp. I was going to have to be careful with my assumptions. "Try for the latter. It might save us some time and energy in the long run."

"I can set the spell to sort out by words."

"Good, try two piles. One for notes that contain the words: treasure, baby, human or amulet. The other for notes that don't."

"Let's hope that we get two piles," Lionel said.

I waited and heard the rustle of paper and bark.

"We've got two piles," Lionel announced. "About even.

"Read some of the ones in the useless pile."

"Why? What will we learn from that to help us with anything?"

I debated just telling him the answer, but I was supposed to be teaching. "What will we learn from the other pile?"

He hesitated and then I heard the humming. He was thinking, which was exactly what I'd hoped.

"We would get information," he finally said. "But we wouldn't know if it was all the information if we just assumed the sorting worked."

I nodded and Lionel started reading. Within two minutes he'd found notes that referred to lost children and lucky pieces.

"Maybe it would help to at least remove the ones we found that don't relate," he suggested. "It will make it easier to sort through."

"No, we need to keep as much useless stuff in each time. But you can mark them with a line if you want to sort them faster." I mentally added statistical analysis to the curriculum. I would have to have him write this stuff down if I was going to be a real teacher.

The next experiment made two piles; one that had any mention of my name or referred to a quest or a job.

This time, I had Lionel check some of the supposedly useful notes. The first one he picked up read *Quinn Larson, when you are done, I have a job for you.* It went on about a related clan who seemed to be enticing the author's mate to move to their territory against her wishes.

"Don't bother going any further." It was time to change tactics.

I heard Lionel shove the notes together again. "I think we need to focus more," he said. "I don't know that we can put so many generalities into the spell and have it work."

"Okay let's focus on the stolen treasure. We can always seek for the other problems later when we have the fairies off our backs."

This time, we asked the spell to pull out any notes that could lead to the recovery of missing treasure with fairy power attached. I figured the babies would still be with the treasure.

"The papers are swirling," Lionel reported. "Do you think the question was too vague?"

I listened to the notes spin, like dry leaves in the fall, they rubbed together and crackled. "Maybe, but it allows the spell to use some logic. What do you know about how sorting spells work?"

"Not much. I don't know if anyone really understands. I just know that if you give the right instructions, a spell can sort through lots of information way faster than any person."

I didn't know much more about it, but I added, "I've done some experiments. If you slow the spell down so you can watch it, you see the same items being checked multiple times. For instance, the spell will look at the notes again after learning information. It can glean meaning with more information."

"You sound like you mean the spell is alive." I heard the interest in his voice. He was hungry for information and being my apprentice seemed to be slowing him down. Helping a blind wizard and investigating problems for fairies wasn't what he needed.

"Kind of," I answered. "Sorting spells are different from any other spell. You always have to contain them within a circle even if you want them to sort things outside the circle. You need to be specific, and you sometimes need to stop them. My theory is they are some kind of spirit."

The whir of objects spinning was still going on ten minutes later. "Um, Quinn?"

"Yes?"

"When will we know to stop the spell?"

"I think we'll give it another ten minutes. Then we'll stop it until we have more time."

A few minutes later the sound stopped. Lionel didn't say anything. "Well what happened?"

He breathed out a long breath. "We have three pieces of paper."

That didn't necessarily mean success. "And?"

"I don't understand why someone wouldn't have given us this information sooner."

"Fairies can be odd about giving information. They are like children sometimes; they just don't think to tell you things."

"These notes are different from the others," he said. "The writing is nicer, and the paper is... I don't know, it's thinner."

"Let's not look for it to be more complicated than it already is. Tell me what the notes say."

"One reads *'It's the sidhe'*, one reads, *'Look in the great park'*, and the other reads *'It's strangers'.*"

. . .

WE WERE STILL TRYING TO FIGURE OUT IF THE RESULTS WERE useful an hour later, while we ate an early dinner.

"It's not new information," I said for what felt like the fiftieth time. An argument that got weaker in my mind every time I said it.

Lionel didn't respond right away, maybe he was smart enough that he realized we needed a different approach. He finally said, "I think we just need to decide whether it worked or not. Unless we test the results, we won't know. What if it worked?"

I decided to stop trying to win the argument and turn it into a teaching moment. "You tell me. If we knew that this information was valid, what difference would it make?"

Lionel started to make his humming sound again. "If we knew it was valid, we could move ahead and stop trying to find a place to start. We could look for some kind of connection between the synymphs – which I think must be the strangers – and the sidhe."

I nodded my agreement, but said, "And if we knew the opposite? You always need to look at all the angles, Lionel. Not just the ones you want to be true."

"Okay, Quinn, but we are not quite back at square one. We know at least three fairies have a theory. We could find out who they are with a regular tracking spell and ask for more information."

"So, either way there's some value in the information. How long will it take you to look through the rest of the notes?"

He groaned. "I was afraid of that. I can scan them in an hour or maybe two. You want me to make sure there are no notes undermining our assumption. Hey, on the bright side, if the information works, you've created a really useful spell."

"You helped. You might as well start on the notes, we can go out after you've finished. I'm sure there are lots more of them waiting at Banks'."

I started clearing the dishes so Lionel could just deal with the notes, when I heard the door bang and a loud groan come from the hall. Lionel brushed my shoulder as he ran to see what was going on.

"Beacon, what happened? Are you all right? No, stupid question, of course you aren't." His babble was cut off by the sound of the door slamming closed.

I felt my way to the hall. "Lionel, for the sake of my sanity, what is going on?"

Beacon groaned again and managed to choke out, "I got jumped... as I was leaving the park." The last words came out on a gasp.

"He's bleeding, Quinn. And he can barely stand." Panic lurked in the words.

"Okay. Put him on the couch." When I heard Lionel grunt, I figured Beacon was safe. I told Lionel to get something to press against the wounds. While he was gone, I ran my hands gently over Beacon's body. "This feels like an interesting story. We'll wait to hear it though. Tell me if anything is actually broken."

"No." He forced out the word and I knew we were losing him to sleep faster than I wanted.

"I brought the towels, is that okay?" Lionel pressed the cloth into my hand.

I pushed it back at him. "The towels are fine, but you need to do it. Press against the wounds, start with the worst. They should close up pretty fast. His blood will form a film over the break as long as we stop it flowing."

Lionel leaned between me and the patient. I stepped back, mindful of the coffee table. It wouldn't do to have me trip over furniture and break a leg.

"It's working. The films are forming." The panic had subsided. "There are some really bad bruises showing up on his arms."

"Don't worry about them, kid," Beacon said his voice already stronger now that the bleeding had stopped. "I'll reabsorb them as soon as I feel better."

"It seems whoever attacked you knew enough to hurt you too

badly to heal yourself, and not badly enough to do permanent damage if you got help," I said. "Lionel, get some of that bread and soak it in beer. It will help him gain his strength."

Beacon grunted.

"Tell me now," I whispered. "While Lionel is busy. Who did this?"

"I didn't see them. But I was told to pass on a message. I guess, I'm part of the message."

"Here's the beer and bread," Lionel announced. "Did you recognize the voice?"

So much for sheltering him from the news. I hoped it wasn't someone he liked, because whoever it was, I planned to return the favor. As soon as I could, I would hurt them, then I would ruin their standing in the Real Folk world.

I heard Beacon suck in some of the food and then Lionel gasp. "Oh! Sprites do heal fast."

"Yes. We do." Beacon's voice was already stronger. "This is going to knock me out for a while, but I'll be fine."

I knew that wasn't a guarantee. Beacon was a long way from fine. In the next couple of hours, he could just as easily fade away as finish healing. "What was the message? Where exactly did it happen?" I needed that before he fell asleep. Knowing sprite physiology, even if he survived it sounded to me like he'd be down until midday tomorrow.

"'Stay out of it, or we'll do a more thorough job,' is the message." Then he gave a loud yawn. "I didn't recognize who, but I'm pretty sure it was sidhe." Then he started snoring.

"Lionel, cover him with a couple of blankets, he needs to stay warm."

There was no reason for us to stay and watch him. If he was going to fade, we could do nothing to stop it. But we could find out where he was jumped with an easy spell. If he was on his way back to me, there were only a few places it could have happened.

CHAPTER 11

An hour later, Lionel was standing beside me in the park. The sounds were muted, and Lionel was silent, so I asked, "Are you ready?"

He kept his response to a "yep", so he didn't break his concentration.

I took a breath and said, "Okay, cast the spell and try to follow it. Don't leave if you lose it. We'll just re-cast. I don't want either of us alone if there is a chance his attackers are still here."

"Done." Lionel put my hand on his arm and started walking. "I put a slow down on the spell. It will stay in sight."

"I didn't know you knew that." Did I have any control over what he learned?

"Oh, yes. I found it in one of your books. It seemed simple. I figured it would work on a spell just as easily as it did on the fly." His voice was nonchalant, but I swore I heard a hint of question.

I wasn't sure I was comfortable with him trying spells even I hadn't thought of doing. "Let's agree you'll keep the experiments to a minimum."

"Okay, I promise," he said a little too easily for my comfort. "It's going into that group of trees beside the mini golf course."

We followed whatever Lionel had used for the spell and came on a clearing, barely larger than a natural space between trees, by the feel of it. I told Lionel to disperse the spell and start searching for anything that might help.

"What kind of thing?"

"Footprints, dropped jewelry, a signed note saying *I did this*. I don't know. Maybe we'll know it when we see it." If I could see it would be so much better, at least for me. "Sorry. I wish I could help."

"I know, why don't I recreate what happened? If you can hear it, then you might get something out of it that I'll miss."

Now he was getting cocky. Recreation spells were complicated. But they tended to either work or not. There would be no unwanted repercussions from a miscast. "Have you tried this on any insects?"

"No. I promise that was just the one time. I did read up on it. I know it's complicated, but..."

"I know. Let's try." I told him to gather some samples of things that got damaged in the beating. "Beacon's blood would be good, but by now the other plants would have drawn it in. Sprite blood is like fertilizer."

I heard him scratching around in the debris from the trees.

"I have a branch that looks broken off recently. There's a scrap of cloth that I think came from Beacon's shirt. And there are a couple of plants that look really healthy – I mean *really* healthy. Do you think I should pick one? It might have Beacon's blood in it."

"No. Picking them will kill them. It's not respectful to waste sprite blood. We can still use them. Put what you have next to one of the healthy plants."

"Should I draw a circle?"

I said no because we didn't need the power of a circle increasing the spell. We just wanted to know what happened recently, not what has been happening since the first sprout took root.

"Are we ready?" Lionel's eagerness was infectious. I suppressed the urge to say yes and had him tell me what he was planning one more time before I gave him the go ahead.

I heard him murmuring the words, and then there was a sudden shift in the background noise. The spell had worked. Now let's see if it worked properly.

There were sounds of someone talking, but everything was muffled. "What can you see?"

Lionel let go of my arm. "Not much. I can make out Beacon, and there are four others. I think there are four, anyway. They keep shifting and stretching. They might be sidhe, but they are all dressed in black."

"Cancel the spell. No need to use up your energy on this." I still strained to make out any words as Lionel did as he was told.

"What did I do wrong?"

"Nothing. There's something in the way of your spell. It's like someone tried to erase the event. I've heard of spells that can do that, but this is the first time I've encountered one."

"Now what?"

Good question. One I didn't have a good answer for. "Take the cloth and the branch. We might be able to get some information off them back in the workshop."

As we walked back to my place, I tried to guess who might have reason to make me stop doing something. Just assuming it was about the fairy treasure was a stupid mistake.

If Beacon was right, and it was sidhe, the most obvious culprits were the twins and Ailin. But that meant they had more followers. If there were really four of them and that wasn't part of the cover spell.

If he was wrong, then it might have been druids. They could use violence to their advantage. And they would know precisely how much damage to do to Beacon. And they would have the power to cast that erasure spell. But why? They would have come looking for the amulet before doing anything else. While they could do violence, they'd learned through their very long lives that violence was more likely to escalate rather than end a problem.

It's possible the druids are taking the treasure. No, that's not how they operate.

I couldn't help remembering four other people I had recently seen. Four people who dressed in black. One of which, at least, was more than she appeared.

"Quinn, I just saw something."

I rubbed my nose which I'd banged into his back when he'd stopped without warning. "You need to be more specific."

"Sorry. I saw a sidhe. It might have been one of the twins." He started walking again and then turned right. "It is one of them. Should we follow?"

"Where are we?" I'd lost track, trusting Lionel to get me home while I followed my thoughts.

"Just outside the park. The twin is walking up Nicola, maybe going in another entrance. Maybe this is how they get in?"

"Go," I gave him a shove. "I'll keep up. If he's alone, we might be able to get some information."

He started to run, and I followed the sound of his footsteps. I didn't run until I felt the bushes on my right. I was on the park side of the street. I was safe from traffic.

"He is going into the park," Lionel called.

"Do you think he saw us?" I managed to pant out.

"No, he's focused on where he's going. Are you going to be okay if the ground gets rough?" I felt him slow a little.

"I'll be fine," I said with all the optimism I could muster. "Keep going."

I tried to keep my sense of direction intact while we ran down the path – thank the spirits it was a path and we weren't trying to force our way through the trees. We were headed towards the back end of the lagoon.

"We are near the synymph trees," Lionel whispered. "This is almost where Dirant and I spent the night."

"How far ahead is the twin?" I worried that we were making too much noise, even though Lionel didn't seem to care.

"Far enough. He's in the trees anyway. His attention is all on not falling down. We might have to go into the trees, but the path leads to the synymph clearing so maybe not."

It's possible that we were looking at things too simply. It might not be the sidhe or the synymphs; it could be they were working together. I was going to have to find out more about these newcomers. Our local nymphs had no desire for treasure and would be unlikely to work with sidhe. The nymphs were tied to the trees and the sidhe usually didn't come near the dirty forest.

"Stop," Lionel whispered, this time before actually stopping, so I avoided another collision.

"What now?" I tried not to sound exasperated, but I was so tired of seeing the world through other people's eyes. I couldn't quite shake the feeling that I would see something they missed.

"Can't you hear that?"

"No." I tried to listen beyond my own ragged breath, and then, just at the edge of it, I heard voices.

"We need more?" The voice was harsh but, I recognized it. Owen apparently was as little used to running as I was.

"Sh," the other voice cut across whatever Owen was saying. "We don't need the whole forest hearing our business."

Then they seemed to stop speaking. Knowing that if we could hear them, they could hear us, I tried to pull Lionel close enough to speak without any volume. He resisted and I let him go. But I wasn't prepared for the fact that he kept going. I heard his footsteps on the dried pine needles. Then nothing. I stood still and hoped I wasn't standing like an idiot in the middle of a jogging trail.

After what felt like a couple of minutes, I decided that I was standing in the middle of the path, so I took a few tentative steps to the left and found a tree trunk to lean against. Then I dug in my pockets and found two spells. One to make me less easy to see, and the other I'd totally forgotten about. It was a long ear. I would be able to hear people talking about half a kilometer away.

I activated both, and then turned my ear toward the direction Lionel had gone. I heard a rush of sound as the spell moved forward. Then a couple of words caught my attention. I re-tuned my hearing.

"If we take more, I don't know if we will get away with it." Owen's voice was a little whinier than before.

"Who will stop us? The stupid fairies don't have guards out, even now." Ailin! I knew it.

"You don't know Quinn Larson. He beat us even without his sight."

That felt good for a second until I realized I should have told Princess to make sure they set guards. Crap, I made a mental note to do it as soon as we got home.

"Yes, I know. But then I wasn't there. If I had been, I'd have stopped you from attacking in an enclosed space. That was a stupid move. What if Maeve had decided to act?" Ailin snapped.

"Who cares what she would have done. She did nothing. When we get—"

"I told you to never mention what we are doing in public!" Ailin's voice burned with anger and some other emotion I couldn't name.

I sympathized with him. The twins could be quite annoying. I hoped Lionel was able to do more than hear the same thing I could. I didn't know where he was, and I couldn't hear any other breathing.

"Okay," Owen whined. "I'll try to get more later. Are they ready to take more?"

"Yes. Shit, what was that?"

"Just some animal?" Owen offered the suggestion like a question. "You aren't used to this wild part of the world."

"Oh, and I suppose you are."

I heard a smack. "You shouldn't hit me. Besides it could be anything."

I hoped that whatever had caught their attention wasn't Lionel. I could hear him breathing now, just at the edge of the conversation. I'm sure it was the spell and they couldn't hear his gentle breath.

Then I heard a crack of some branch snapping and then Ailin said, "Shit, it's him. Run."

Then all I heard was the sound of two people running for their lives. I guessed it wasn't Lionel that frightened them off. By the slow beat of his heart, he wasn't that frightened himself.

I let the spells go and waited for Lionel to return.

"Moss showed up," he announced. "He said he'd make sure they left. I told him about Beacon."

Oh no. "What exactly did you tell him?"

"Just what we know. I said we don't know who did it. Um, I didn't want to send him after the sidhe unless we knew for sure."

"No. You did the right thing." I didn't want to do that either. "The only thing we know is that they are stealing the treasure."

"How did you know?"

I told him about the long ear, and he sighed. "So, you heard everything."

"Not everything and I didn't see anything. I heard everything after Owen said they might get caught if they took more. 'More' I think means the treasure."

"They were just talking up to then. Although Ailin said he was going to refresh the repel charm. I guess they are keeping the forest people away. If Moss hadn't shown up, we might have heard where they're putting the treasure."

I wasn't sure about that. Ailin was pretty cautious.

"We could go tell Maeve?" Lionel's tone was reluctant, and I agreed that he had right to be.

"No. Princess asked us to find and return the treasure. If Maeve acts too soon, they will never tell where the treasure is. And we may never learn why they wanted it in the first place."

Lionel started leading me back the way we had come. "I think we know it's buried, or stored, here in the park."

"It's a big park." I didn't relish the idea of searching for hidden treasure in Stanley Park; four hundred and five hectares of mostly forest.

"I know, but the spell said the synymphs were involved. How much territory do you think they control?"

"It didn't say the synymphs, it said strangers. But I'll give you the fact that the spell worked. Two out of the three notes are right."

He started moving faster. "We can try to trace the fairies that dropped off each of the notes. Maybe they can give more information." Lionel was really anxious to use a tracing spell.

"Slow down. The notes will still be there." He slowed a little, but we were still almost trotting.

"Quinn, we may have solved one case."

One case? Great. Quinn Larson, wizard, and personal investigator. "Not a case, Lionel, just someone's problem." I sped up anyway. I was as eager as he was to find out if we were about to get the fairies off our backs. And I wanted to check on Beacon. He should be recovering, but I wasn't sure how Moss would react if his grandson didn't heal. Moss could just as easily hold me responsible for Beacon's health, as the people who beat him up.

By the time we turned into my front yard, I was panting, had a stitch in my side, and had decided to start getting back into shape.

CHAPTER 12

When we got through the door, I checked on Beacon. His breathing was good, and he seemed to be deeply asleep. It looked like the danger had passed.

I got my breath back while Lionel made some clove tea. I could smell the healing properties of the steam from the couch.

"I need to change." Lionel said.

I heard him head towards me. I held up my hand and said, "I'm good. I managed to pick what I'm wearing right now so I should be okay."

"Um... Are you sure?"

"What? I'm wearing a tee-shirt and jeans." I touched both articles of clothing. Yes, soft cotton of the tee-shirt and rough denim.

"Well, that's not quite all."

I groaned. "Stop being kind. Tell me."

"Your jeans are green, and the shirt is purple. You look kind of odd."

"Okay, come with me and we'll sort the clothes to match. Then I am dressing myself. I'll live with the combinations I come up with even if they're bad." I thought about that for a minute. "I mean I'll live with it unless we're going to court. I am not wearing blind guy colors in front of the sidhe in their finery."

We sorted my wardrobe into matching clothes. There were two columns of shelves. Anything in the same column went together. What I tried to ignore is the pile of clothes I knew were still on the floor. What the heck could I have bought that couldn't sort onto one of the shelves?

"They don't really go with anything," Lionel told me. "I think they're very old."

I just ignored him and sent him out so I could dress. "From now, on I'll only buy black clothes," I vowed.

When I returned to the living room, Lionel drew me to the counter and we shared a snack.

"I think we should try to talk to Princess," he said. "There are too many holes in our information. I don't know if we can solve this case without understanding more about the fairy treasure."

"It's not a case. We're solving a problem." He was right though. Without information, I didn't know where to look for motives. And I was starting to worry about the babies. How long could they survive without food?

I put down my fork and told him, "Send out a call. You do know how to do that, right?"

"Yes." He was eager again. Ah to be so young. "Do you want to supervise?"

I considered it, but he needed to feel confident without me watching his every move; or listening to it anyway. And I had his vow. And I had really strong protections. If he cast the spell wrong, I could banish whatever came before it was a problem. "No. Go ahead."

I heard him clomp down the stairs. And then clomp back up. "You can't have done it already."

"Uh, I need access to some thorns. You have them sealed away."

He'd need more than thorns, so I released the protections on all the ingredients so he wouldn't have to keep coming up every time he needed something. "You have fifteen minutes. If you haven't gathered your ingredients by then, the seals will go back on."

"Thanks, Quinn. I'll be fine." He clomped back down to the workroom.

In ten minutes, I heard a bang, an 'oops', and then he came back up. "She'll be here in a few minutes. I cleaned up."

I laughed. "I bet you did."

"She's kind of mad I called her." He was trying to sound uncaring, but I heard the tremor of fear in his voice.

"I'll fix it. She wants our help, so she should expect to come when we need her."

"Brave words my friend," Beacon muttered before turning over and going back to sleep. I hoped he was dreaming, and not responding to what I said.

Princess knocked, and when Lionel let her in, he was careful to say 'this one time'. She sniffed before saying "Of course."

"Do not drop anything in my house," I called to her. "If you do, you are giving me a gift, not planting permission."

I felt a tiny hand caress my face. "Clever wizard, I will behave. Why did you call me here? Do you have my treasure?"

It bugged me that she didn't ever ask 'do you have my babies'. "We are close. We need more information."

Her hand left my cheek abruptly.

She hissed. "What information? I cannot give you clan secrets."

"We need to know what value someone would place on your babies, or your treasure. Well, value other than the face value. There must be something more than the obvious."

Princess paused. Then she said, "I need the oath of everyone that they will not tell this information."

I nodded. "You have my oath that what you tell us will not be shared. But, Princess, someone knows. That's why they took your treasure."

"I need them to give their oath as well. I do not know who has told the secret, but it will not be my fault." She waited.

Lionel gave his oath, but I didn't know how we were going to get it from Beacon. "Don't wake him," I cautioned in case anyone was moving to the couch. "If he does not heal, Moss will want to know why."

I heard Princess take in a breath. "Is that the heir?"

"What heir?" Lionel blurted out.

"Moss is grooming someone to take responsibility for the forest," she whispered. "His grandson."

Moss only had one grandson, so I guess the answer was yes. "It's Beacon."

"I do not need his oath. He has already sworn to protect the park and all creatures associated with it. That means all the fairies."

I'd be following up on that little snippet of information when we were done with all our problems. "So why would someone want your treasure, and your babies?"

She jumped onto my lap. "The babies are incidental, Quinn. I know you think I am heartless, but it's the treasure that is important."

I waited and tried to convey to Lionel that he shouldn't interrupt.

"We put our babies in the treasury to quicken them. Until they absorb enough power, they are just dormant. Like a cater-pillar in its cocoon. Our babies will be fine for days yet. The trea-sure is soaked with fairy power. It takes it from around us."

"Another battery." I had a sinking feeling I knew why Ailin wanted as much treasure as he could get his hands on. And, if the babies were cocoons mixed with the treasure, he wouldn't have bothered sorting them out.

"Yes," Princes said, jumping down from my lap. "Someone is using our power to fuel something. Anything needing that much power will be bad for fairies. And any other Real Folk, I think."

Oh, not all of the Real Folk, but a couple of wizards and a sidhe Queen. "Thank you, Princess."

"You can thank me by returning what belongs to the fairies. If you need me again, use this." She put an acorn into my hand. "Just flick the cap off and say my name. No need to compel me again."

Before I could apologize, and say we only intended to request her presence, the door slammed.

"Lionel, how did you compel her?"

He coughed, and then said, "I may have used too much thorn. Oh well, no harm done."

No, but that was only luck.

I checked Beacon again, now that I knew he was Moss's heir I felt a bit more terrified of the repercussions. He was breathing deeply. That meant his healing was complete and now he just needed to sleep.

"Are you up to trying to see Maeve?" I asked Lionel.

"What about the twins? How will we get past them?"

"I don't know. We'll think of something when we get there." I picked my coat up from the chair. I was getting really good at remembering where things were. It felt like progress. Then I barked my shins on the stool I'd just been sitting on.

"Let's at least go look and see what's happening. If the twins are around, we can try to get someone in there to let her know we need to talk to her." There was always the tunnel. Maybe we could sneak in the back door.

"Okay," Lionel said as he helped me shrug into my coat.

We opened the door and I went to step through, but Lionel stood in my way. "Now what?"

"Druids." In that one word, Lionel managed to convey awe and terror. Although I guess the emotions are similar enough.

"Quinn Larson, please allow us past your wards. We wish to talk."

"Please be welcome in my home," I said automatically. Almost as if they made me say it.

We went back to the living room and I heard Lionel fussing to make the druids at home. "We need nothing, apprentice."

The druids sounded as though they were speaking from the end of a long tunnel. I guess it helped with the mysterious reputation. I tried not to allow myself to be impressed.

"What can I do for you?" I asked, keeping my voice as respectful as I could make it. I really needed to let Maeve know what we'd found out about Ailin. So, I wanted this over as quickly as possible.

"We are aware that you are in a hurry, wizard, so we will be brief." I thought it was the same druid speaking every time, but the sound came from different directions. Maybe all druids sounded the same, or maybe they were playing tricks on the blind wizard.

"Okay, I am happy to hear you out." I figured it was about the amulet, but since I had to play for time, I was going to make them actually ask for it. And if it wasn't about the amulet, I didn't want to bring the subject up.

"We are aware of many things that happen outside the walls of our museum."

If they thought being brief was speaking in one sentence pronouncements, we were in for a long night. "Anything in particular of interest lately?"

"A great deal." I heard a quick whispered conversation. "Perhaps we should be plain."

"That would be nice." If they didn't get to the point soon, I was going to throw up from the tension.

"My brother druid suggests that we may be of mutual value to each other."

That was a relief. I was expecting a threat, something on the order of 'give us our amulet, or we will confine your soul to eternal labor'. "I'm always happy to help."

"Perhaps some tea?" Lionel was far more gracious than I was.

"We have already declined. There is nothing we need to facilitate our conversation."

Before Lionel could react, I said, "Let's get down to business, gentlemen. We all have places to go."

Another whispered conversation.

Then one of them said, "We need to retrieve the amulet. The souls are becoming more restless every day. For this we will exchange information." The words came from someone on my left.

"I have started the process to retrieve the amulet from where I hid it," I said.

An identical voice from my right side said, "Why did you not return it to our museum when you retrieved it?"

Did they really think it was safe there? "I wasn't sure it would be secure. I was worried that someone else would try to use it."

"So, you felt it necessary to hide our amulet, the repository of druid souls, somewhere we were not able to locate it?" I stopped turning my head toward the voices.

"Well it was safe where we put it. And when you told Lionel you wanted it back, I arranged for secure passage. Why are the souls becoming restless, anyway?"

"We do not know. And it is not your concern. When do you expect to receive the amulet?"

I couldn't resist the opportunity to get a few tidbits of information. The druids knew a lot of lore others had forgotten even existed. I wasn't going to hold the amulet hostage exactly, but if it wasn't for me, the amulet would still be in Fionuir's hands.

"My apprentice was impressed with his visit to your museum. I think, maybe, his specialty will be found in the study of history."

"We are happy to provide access to our library for a willing student." More whispers. "In return for the amulet, we will be happy to provide him with twelve hours of instruction."

Nice, but I thought it was worth more than that. "I have some current problems you might help me with."

"We may be able to help with your problems, but we are not a database for your ongoing use."

I was getting too close to a line I didn't relish crossing. I backed off a bit. "No, I would never expect you to be. I think, perhaps, I am surprised that you have ventured from your museum twice in the last two days, and yet in the last ten years, no one has seen a druid inside, or outside, the museum."

"Times change and with it we must change. You know that, Quinn Larson."

Why did that sound ominous? "Should we be preparing for something? Like a war?" I hoped not. Wars were difficult things among the Real Folk. It was often impossible to know who was on whose side − it changed sometimes by the hour. And in the end, no one was sure of anyone. They always cost lives, and they sometimes came very close to exposing us to the humans.

"It is too soon to tell. The signs are, as yet, unclear."

No one spoke for a few minutes after that.

Beacon groaned in his sleep but didn't wake. Lionel started drumming his fingers on the counter, and the druids started whispering again. I was getting tired of the silence but didn't know how to break it.

The problem with druids is that they can make the most mundane statement seem like a weighty pronouncement of doom. If a druid said good morning, most people started wondering when the trouble would start. When they went into retreat ten years ago, there were a lot of people who felt nothing but an overwhelming relief.

The druid finally spoke. "We must come to some agreement."

"It's not a problem. As soon as I get the amulet back, I'll hand it over. If you are going to take care of it, I don't need to worry." It actually felt good to realize I wouldn't be responsible for such a powerful battery.

"It would be foolish of you to do otherwise, wizard."

Silence again. This time I broke it. "So, we will see you in two days?"

"We are not finished."

CHAPTER 13

I t was getting too late to drop in on the court now anyway, so I might as well hear them out. "What else is there to say?"

"We did not wish to be in your debt, and yet we find ourselves there."

Again with the one sentence conversations. I just waited until they were ready to continue. And I hoped Lionel would relax soon. The finger drumming was driving me crazy. Beacon turned over on the couch. And finally, the druid spoke again.

"We are in your debt twice over. You rescued the druid souls from the sidhe Queen. You placed it in a safe location until we were ready to receive it."

I nodded.

"We are prepared to give you information that will aid you in your current quests. Will that satisfy the debt?"

I thought it over and decided it couldn't hurt to have some druid advice, even if it was likely to be more of a puzzle than a clear direction. "I believe so. If the information is useful, yes. If there is a trick, then no. And I believe that will mean you owe me a further debt."

The whispering started again.

Finally, my answer came. "We will provide three pieces of information. One of them will be false. When we receive the amulet, we will tell you which is false. Is this arrangement satisfactory?"

Since I had no intention of double crossing them, it worked for me. "Yes."

"Very well. The first information relates to the fairy treasure. You now know that the treasure is a battery, yes?"

"I just found out, yes. And it worries me."

"The amount of treasure they are amassing will soon be sufficient to break your confinement of Fionuir."

Oh great, I am about to face a vengeful sidhe. I could always hope that was the false information. "How soon?"

"That is not information we have to share."

I noted the phrasing and guessed they knew but weren't going to share. "Okay, I guess it means we need to move faster."

"The next piece of information is for your personal quest. There is a human child who is not what she seems."

"Yes, I've seen her."

"Do not interrupt."

I apologized.

"We do not have all the details. But we do know that someone is protecting her. We believe it is because she was part of the demon summoning that it succeeded. And we believe that she does not know what happened."

Not new information, but confirmation of what we'd guessed. I really hoped that wasn't the false information. "And the third?"

"For that I must touch you. Do I have your permission?"

"Sure," I said. If the druids had meant me harm, they would have already done it.

I felt the dry touch of old skin on my forehead and tried not to flinch. I heard a rush of voices and then silence. "I have given you a spell that will save a life. You will be able to access it with the word 'mnemonic'."

"Thank you." I didn't know what else to say.

I heard a flurry of cloth robes, and then the door open and close. Lionel returned already talking, "That was so cool. I can't believe you got three pieces of information from the druids. Hey, do you think they will follow through on the offer to give me lessons?"

I laughed. "Slow down. First of all, I only got two pieces of information. And since I don't know which is false, it might as well be no information until I hand over the amulet."

"Oh, yeah. Well, I guess..." His enthusiasm was fading, and I took pity on him.

"If you want them to, the druids will teach you. That's what they do. They teach. You just need to ask. Do you want to ask?"

"Well, as long as you are okay with it. Yes, I would like to spend time with them."

I was okay with it. I wasn't okay with him waiting for me to be okay. "Lionel, it's up to you. If you want to find knowledge elsewhere, just tell me. I won't stand in your way. In fact, I probably know the best teacher in any topic you want to know. Being an apprentice is not indentured servitude."

"Then I'll go ask," he said. "But I'll wait until they have the amulet back, just in case."

I laughed. "Maybe you can teach me something when you start your lessons."

"Um, that's nice, but you know way more than me." He gave a little cough and then said, "Should we go see Maeve now?"

I shook my head. "It's too late. If we go now, we might have to wake her up. That's not going to help her listen."

"But the treasure is almost enough to free Fionuir."

I understood his impatience. "Almost is not the same as enough. I don't think they'll be able to take any more tonight, since we suggested Princess set guards. And remember it might not be true."

"Yes, but even if it's not true, that might be a bad thing. Not true could mean there's not enough, or that they already have enough."

Sometimes his logic really didn't help me sleep at night.

CHAPTER 14

Beacon woke up around ten the next morning feeling healthier and famished. We fed him and brought him up to date before heading down to the sidhe court.

Because it was noon, and there would be humans around, we needed to disguise Beacon. As much as Lionel needed to practice his magic, I needed to practice doing it blind, so I set the glamour. When I was done, Lionel and Beacon told me it was just like Beacon normally looked but with a dark suntan. Lionel added, "You know, you just need someone to confirm your spells worked. You don't need..."

"Lionel, cut it out. I need you as much as you need me. I don't want to talk about it anymore. I'm going to learn how to get by so I can teach you, not so I can get rid of you." I hadn't meant that to sound so harsh, but I wasn't going to stop learning how to get on by myself. "Sorry."

"That's okay, Quinn," Lionel's voice was stiff. "You are right. I won't mention it again."

I opened my mouth to try to heal the pain I'd just caused, but Beacon whispered, "Let it be. The lad will get over it. He knows what you meant."

I nodded and we set out.

We stopped on the corner opposite the court so that Lionel could check who was at the door. I had high hopes that the twins didn't work morning and evening. I was tired of the hard work of getting past them

"The door is unguarded." Lionel's whisper was tight with tension.

Beacon hmmd before saying, "Probably just stepped away for some reason. There's always two guards."

"We should go now." I started forward, and then a hand pulled me back.

"Quinn, the traffic won't stop in time," Lionel said.

I took a breath. Apparently, I was more eager to get this done than I thought.

"We'll go now," Beacon said. "Lionel first, then you. I'll watch our backs."

I heard the cooing of the traffic signal before I got the tug to start walking. With Lionel in front leading me and Beacon's touch on my shoulder, it felt like we were mounting a campaign to breach a fort, not visit someone who was supposed to be an ally.

"Still no sign of guards," Lionel reported. "The door is open."

I felt the change in the air as we walked down the corridor. The scent of cloves came wafting on a warm draft from ahead. No one challenged us and I was feeling off kilter. It was as if this welcoming feeling was a trap.

Beacon tapped my shoulder. "We're here."

The sound of laughter greeted us as the doors opened.

"Ah, Quinn, welcome. I apologize that no one was there to greet you." Ailin sounded cheerful and threatening all at the same time.

The clove came from him. There was something earthy and damp underneath it. I had a sudden realization that the cloves were there to cover up the other odor. I wondered why he didn't just wash it off.

I pretended his welcome was sincere and expressed my concern. "It is unusual for the Queen to leave the door open to all. What is to stop a human wandering in?"

"Oh, do not fear. The door is warded against vermin." I could hear the smirk sliding across his words like slime.

"We are here to speak to Maeve." I was not going to engage in a verbal battle on his home ground. "We have information she will find valuable." Okay, maybe a little jab.

Beacon whispered, "She is not here. We should go."

I shook my head just a little. It was worth waiting. If Ailin was in a chatty mood, maybe I could get him to betray himself.

"You heard the sprite," Ailin said. "The queen is not here. If you must see her, then you must return at some other time."

Snotty little bastard. "Is she expected soon?"

I felt a brush of lace against my hand and knew Ailin was trying to intimidate me. I couldn't resist. I sniffed and then wrinkled my nose. "Is there a problem with the plumbing?"

I heard a gasp from Lionel and got ready to duck. But nothing happened.

Ailin sighed and said, "She does not share her schedule with me. I think you should leave and return later; perhaps when Owen and Garnet are there to give you a proper greeting."

It was time for discretion. I turned, hoping that Lionel and Beacon were following me. My nose was starting to drip from the smell of damp that came from Ailin. I was pretty sure I'd gotten to him, because the smell had become overwhelming as his stress rose.

"Not so fast, wizard." Ailin placed his hand on my arm.

I flicked the hand away. "Do not touch me."

"Be aware of where you are," Ailin hissed. "This is my home and you will be respectful. Or perhaps you will lose more than just that witch."

I sensed Beacon and Lionel move to my side and tried to keep my temper under control. "She was worth this whole court. If you speak of her again, I will send you to join her on the other side."

I felt Lionel and Beacon tense for a fight and patted the air to calm them. "Do not threaten me or my friends, sidhe. I am very aware that I am in Maeve's court. She would not appreciate you taking ownership."

"Perhaps it will not be her home for much longer," he said it so quietly I don't think anyone else heard.

I took a step, hoping I was facing the door. A touch on my elbow turned me slightly and I was able to walk away with at least a little dignity.

As we stepped back out into the noise of traffic, I heard a snicker cut off by the noon horn. It seemed the twins were back in place.

We made it across the intersection before I felt half safe to talk. "We'll go back later this evening. Maeve is unlikely to stay away from the court for too long."

"Quinn," Lionel said. "I have a theory."

I heard the chatter of humans coming from every direction in search for lunch. I felt dizzy with all the information coming at me after the cloying scents in the sidhe court. "Later. We need to get out of here and figure out what the hell is going on."

Since so many humans were out on the streets, Beacon suggested we head to Banks' before going home. "A beer would be just the thing to wash out that smell." I guess he was feeling better if he was craving a drink.

"Sure, but no more than two. I don't want to go back to the court with a skin full. I'm not sure I could be civil."

Lionel barked a laugh. "That was you being civil?"

I tried on a look of surprised hurt, but I'm not sure from their laughter that I was successful.

"We're here," Beacon said as he swerved right. I'd become much better at reacting to sudden moves of the person leading me. It worked better when I held their elbow, but sometimes it made more sense for someone to pull me along. This time, it meant that I stumbled at the change in direction.

"I'm sorry. I keep forgetting," Beacon said.

"Beacon, don't worry. I'm fine." Something flitted past my cheek. It felt like only the tiniest hairbreadth came between me and something made of terror. I turned my face up and shouted, "Morrigan!"

"The glamour is gone," Lionel shouted. "Beacon, get inside."

Beacon let go of my arm and I felt Lionel move to my side. This flurry of activity had turned my sense of direction on its head. "Just stop for a minute," I said. "Beacon, you go ahead and get out of sight. We can deal with her." What I meant was she'd let us deal with it or we'd be dead, it wasn't really up to us.

A buzz of conversation came and then was cut off as Beacon entered the bar.

I reached out a hand. "Lionel?" He'd moved away and I didn't know where he was.

"Here," his voice came from my right. "She's on the roof ridge across the way."

I look a deep cleansing breath. The Morrigan was up to something but, with her you can never tell what. And good or bad was a little fuzzy where she was concerned. "Face me toward her."

Lionel touched my left shoulder and gave it a push. "You have your back to Banks' door. She's about twenty feet up, right in front of you."

"Morrigan?" I wondered what shape she had taken. Although it was probably crow. If she was the woman, Lionel wouldn't be speaking so clearly. I had seen her in the form of her sexual aspect, and it would make a strong man weep with desire.

All I heard was a caw. A caw that carried the cries of the defeated on the battlefield. The echoes of ages of misery and pain set my nerves on edge.

"What do you want of me?" I pushed a little. The thing to

remember when dealing with any of the death and procreation deities is you don't have any control of what will happen. So, you might as well go on the offensive – respectfully.

"She isn't looking down here," Lionel breathed into my ear. "I, um." He blew out a gust of air. I guessed she'd changed into the woman.

"Don't look," I advised, knowing it wouldn't be easy. This was the first time I was almost glad to be blind. "You go inside if you need to. Just come back out for me."

"I...hoo...I'm fine."

I grinned. "Back to crow, huh?"

He laughed. "It doesn't mean we're safer, but at least I can think."

"We'll have to compare impressions later." I brought my attention back to the current problem. "Is she still there?"

"Yes, but she's still looking at something across the street. Let me see if I can figure out what it is."

I felt his presence shift away.

Another caw filled with pain and terror came from above. It sounded like she was still on the ledge, but the agony echoing through her voice meant she was agitated. I couldn't understand why she didn't just talk to me.

"I can't see anything," Lionel said. "It looks like she's focused on the court, but it is the same as it was when we arrived."

"Morrigan, what do you want us to do?" I didn't know how I was going to add her problems to the list I already couldn't solve, but you didn't refuse The Morrigan.

"Duck!"

I hit the ground without a thought. The touch of her feather had turned Olan from a pixie to a chickadee. And he considered himself lucky.

A breeze blew my hair back and then I felt the weight of a thousand years of sorrow lift from my shoulders.

"She is gone." Lionel's words were unnecessary.

I picked myself up. "Let's go inside. Now I need something stronger than a beer."

We went in and I felt the warmth of all kinds of Real Folk laughing, and arguing, and just being alive. I asked Mark for a double shot of whiskey and leaned against the bar.

CHAPTER 15

We got home a couple of hours, and more than a couple of drinks, later. I'd eventually gotten Lionel and Beacon to give up on trying to figure out what The Morrigan was doing. She would make sure we got her message if it was important. If not, it was just a distraction.

"I think we need to dig a bit more into that human girl. I can't do it, but anyone who can hide in the shadows and trees could follow her." That description would fit any number of Real Folk, including Beacon, if they were disguised well enough. "I am pretty sure we can find her at that bar again. They seemed comfortable there."

"I suppose that's me," Beacon said. "I don't see Lionel lurking successfully in a laurel bush. He's more likely to trip over his large feet and bring attention, than avoid it."

I agreed but didn't say so: "Yes, I meant you."

"Quinn, I've been thinking," Lionel butted in. "I think Ailin might have messed up tonight."

"When, exactly?" I hoped he would give me something concrete. I didn't like the distraction.

"Something he said... I think. It's just... I don't know. We should try to figure out what he meant by that comment." He was frustrated and it didn't help him communicate.

I reminded myself he was my apprentice and it was my responsibility to help him grow. "What comment? The fact that Maeve might not be at home in the court much longer?"

"Yes," Lionel's tone was victorious. Like I got it and would then work out the solution to the problem.

Before I could try to say something to convince him that it meant nothing we didn't know, without being dismissive, Beacon said, "We know he's trying to get Fionuir back. That's not news."

"I know," Lionel said. "But I don't understand why Fionuir's return would banish Maeve."

I was amazed that his keen mind had such difficulty dealing with politics. "They were rivals. When Fionuir returns, they will continue their fighting."

"Yes, but... well, why would Fionuir automatically get control of the court? If they only vote for Queen every fifty years, Maeve has plenty of time to solidify her position."

"Hmm, good point. We'll come back to that after we've sorted out a plan for the human girl." As I said the words, something niggled at the back of my mind. I tried to pull it out, but nothing came. "It will be okay."

"Maeve can look after herself," Beacon said. "At least for a while. If we are going to try to get the human alone, we need to figure out the best timing. I can't just hang around there waiting. Even if I could pass for human, I can't just hang around a group of teenagers. They tend to look closely at men who look like they are in their thirties watching teenage girls. And, I don't have to remind you I look like a sprite; bark-like skin."

It was something to take up Lionel's time. "There's a spell I can cast on a charm. It's probably something like the girl has. It will hold the glamour for a couple of days." It made me think; perhaps someone was refreshing a spell every few days. A lot of work, but if the reason was critical... And if the druids knew about it, it probably was.

"I'll go find the spell," Lionel said, resignation weighing down his words.

I almost promised to follow up on the Ailin thing, but I clamped down on the response. I needed to get something off my to-do list. The teenager seemed the easiest right now.

"So, what do I do?" Beacon asked over the sound of Lionel's trudge down the stairs. "Say I find her. Should I try to ask her about her life?"

"Just find out where she lives. I think we can try to contact her without alarming everyone. She said she had foster parents. Maybe we can find out who she really is somehow." I was already trying out what I'd say. *Hey, so do you know any witches? No, not Wiccan, real witches.* Or, maybe, *Hi I'm a wizard, know any fairies?* Hopefully, I'd come up with something better when we did meet.

"Do you know any way for us to uncover her glamour caster?" Beacon asked.

"All my ideas involve having access to too many different people." I tried not to worry that we were doing a lot of 'figuring it out when it happens' planning.

Lionel clomped up the stairs. "I've got the right book, but some of the ingredients are behind your wards."

"Tell me what you need, and it will be ready before you go back down there." Lionel read a list of about twenty spices and herbs. "I will be back soon," he said.

While he gathered what we needed, Beacon and I finalized our plans. He'd go back to the Goth bar and watch until they left. He'd follow the girl until she went home. "I need to let Moss know I won't be around for a few days," Beacon said. "I'll be back as soon as I can."

· · ·

"You need to go help Lionel," Beacon said when he returned. "I can follow the girl as long as I can stay in cover. But if I need someone to take over, you won't be able to do it."

I knew he was right, but I hated feeling like I wasn't contributing. "I'll help him, don't worry. It would be better if I could get another hour of sight."

"You can't. I spoke to Moss and he said that spell is dangerous. You probably had a lucky break not dying the first time." Beacon grunted and I tried to picture what he was doing. Something must have shown on my face because he said, "I brought some props. I figured if I look like I'm working on something, it wouldn't be as suspicious as if I just hung around. I brought some gardening stuff."

I was impressed. I admit I'd been worrying about him being noticed.

"What do you have?" I asked.

I heard some clanking and then he said, "I have a big pair of scissors. I think they are for trimming dead branches. And this thing I'm supposed to strap on my back, and then I press this button."

Right after he said 'button', I heard a click then a tremendous roaring of a leaf blower. Wind rushed past my face and I was getting ready to throw a kill power spell when it stopped.

"Wow, sorry," Beacon said. "I see how it works, but how do humans stand the noise?"

"They argue about it, but raking leaves is a lot of work." I started patting the surfaces around me. "How much damage did it do?"

"Nothing that Lionel can't clear up in a few minutes."

The clanking started again. "Do you think it will be okay to use this at night?"

"I think it will be more useful for you to be seen carrying a toolkit. I have one somewhere around here. You can be a workman going home. It will make you look more legitimate." As long as no one gets too close.

"But think about how much I can tidy up with this," Beacon's voice was wistful. "Won't the humans be happy if their leaves were all brushed away in secret?"

"How did you plan to use that in secret?" I didn't want to take away his toy, but there was no way he could be stealthy if he was blowing garden trash around every five minutes.

"Don't you have a spell that could muffle the noise?"

"Nothing that we can put together quickly," I said.

Lionel clomped back up the stairs, cutting off whatever rationalization Beacon could try next. "It's all ready for us to cast. Do you want to come down?"

I nodded and started to go towards the basement when I had a thought. "Beacon, how did you get that equipment?"

"One of the wood imps. He liberated it from the park gardeners. I have to get it back in a couple of days or they'll miss it. Why?"

"I was just wondering if they set you up for failure, but I don't know why a wood imp would do that. Do you know which one?"

"Yes, Liantry. She owes Moss a few favors so he had her find me a disguise."

"I guess if she was repaying a favor for Moss, she was just misguided." I wasn't sure if my suspicions were really allayed, but I let it go.

Downstairs, Lionel talked me through the position of all the ingredients.

"Okay, can you find something we can use to hold the spell?" I ran the positions through my mind again. From the right six bowls: myrrh, clay, cranberry juice, salt, sage, and mint.

"Here's a hazelnut," Lionel said.

I placed it in the empty bowl in front of me. "Do you know where my tools are?" I asked Lionel.

"Upstairs in the bathroom. I was trying to fix the dripping tap. Shall I get them?"

I heard a bit of disappointment in his voice. I thought about how I was going to manage the spell. It was tricky to apply the ingredients and I probably would have difficulty making sure I didn't spill anything.

"Not yet. You can get it when Beacon leaves, and you can take the bag he brought back to the park." I stepped away. "Right now, you'll need to set the spell. Are you ready?"

"Yes, thank you, Quinn."

We all calmed our thoughts and waited until Lionel told us he was ready to start. He spoke the words and I pictured the progress of the spell; a touch of myrrh to coat the nut, then a roll in the clay pot to mimic the smooth color of skin, one drop of cranberry juice which honored Beacon's heritage of wood and bogs. Then the salt to disturb people's eyes, the sage to protect against counter spells and the mint to freshen the scent of the mixture.

"Okay," Lionel said. "Beacon, if you take this, we should... I mean I should be able to see the evidence."

I waited a few seconds and then said, "Well?"

"It seems to be working, but would I notice if it didn't?" Lionel asked.

"There's a mirror upstairs. If the spell took, Beacon should be able to tell."

I heard two sets of feet charge up the stairs and carefully followed.

"It's odd to see myself like this," Beacon said, "I look like I'm sickening for something."

"Why, what happened?" I immediately started trying to think of a counter spell I could set.

"I'm a kind of tan color, all over. No tracings. When we sicken, we fade like this. Why didn't you just make me dark like before?"

Lionel gave a little cough before answering. "Well, I thought it might work better if we did something less intense. If the color is lighter, it will take less power to keep it going longer. I can change it if you like."

"No, it's just weird to look ill," Beacon said.

My apprentice was full of surprises. "That was good thinking, Lionel. Now grab the toolbox so Beacon can get going."

Lionel and Beacon left at the same time. Beacon told him how to return the gardening equipment and promised to contact us as soon as he had some information.

While Lionel was gone, I fumbled around the kitchen tidying up. I wasn't sure how useful it was, but I needed to fill the time. I moved on to the living room and picked up a number of papers that the leaf blower had strewn around. Then the door opened, and, since he was the only person who could come and go as he pleased, I assumed Lionel was back.

"It's done," he called before slamming the door shut.

"Now we just need to wait, I think." I handed him the papers I held.

He took them and I heard some rustling that I assumed was him picking up more from the floor.

"I've been thinking, Quinn," he said.

I bit back the sarcastic comment, trying to remember how I'd hurt his feelings yesterday, and gestured for him to continue. I guess he was looking because he said, "About Ailin."

"What about him?"

"I think I may have figured out where the treasure is. At least, more or less where it is."

I nodded. Ailin was cocky, so he may have let something slip that I couldn't see. Something that only Lionel might have understood the meaning of.

He continued, "I think he was trying to cover up that smell. That's why there was so much incense going. I thought I would gag on the cloves. Do you want some tea, or a sandwich?"

"I'm fine, but you go ahead and get something to eat," I said, then changed the subject back to Ailin. "What do you think it means?"

He opened cupboards and I heard him take the lid off a jar. "I think it will tell us where he has the treasure hidden. I think he was not the only one in the room covering up that smell."

"There are spells that can locate places by samples of things." I started trying to think of spells that might work on a description of a scent. That would be hard, but I think Ailin would notice if we tried a tracer spell on him.

"You mean like we get a sample of mud from his shoes and we can find out where the mud came from?" Lionel's words came through a mouthful of food. "How are we going to get some of the stuff that smells so bad?"

"We can't take the chance that he'll catch us. Did you happen to notice who else had the smell on them?" I tried not to feel annoyed that I should have noticed it. I really had to work on paying attention to everything around me, not just whoever was trying to yank my chain.

Lionel pushed his plate across the counter before saying, "No, he didn't let anyone else get close to us. If we can find out, we can get the treasure back, right?"

I had a flash of Lionel sneaking up behind a sidhe and trying to scrape a sample of dirt off their clothes. "Yes, but let's not take too many risks. If we get caught by Ailin, he won't give us a second chance."

"Okay," he sighed out the word. "It was a pretty earthy smell. Maybe we can find the place by sniffing around the park. It's probably in the park, right?"

"Since we heard him there, I think that's a good bet." I remembered what Ailin had said to me before we left, *'change comes when you least expect it'*.

The bits of information all added up in my mind, suddenly.

"He thinks he is almost ready. He is feeling cocky. Maybe we can prod him into getting careless."

"I could keep an eye on him. Maybe find out where he goes," Lionel said.

That was not a safe plan. It was more likely to get Lionel captured and held in some hole in the wall until Ailin finished bringing Fionuir back. Even if Lionel was careful, I was pretty sure that Ailin would notice a tall skinny redhead following him around. "We need to find a way to make him do something in front of Maeve that opens the door for our accusation. If she hears him talk and we can make him say something stupid, she'll stop him. If he starts threatening me, I can accuse him of trying to bring Fionuir back." I tried to feel as confident as I sounded, but it didn't work.

Lionel yawned. "I'm wiped out. Do you want to go to the court tonight?"

It was tempting, but we were both exhausted. Me from fretting, and Lionel from casting what was a pretty complex spell. "I need to think this over. Remember one of the things we were told was not true. We are reading Ailin's behavior as though the druids told the truth about Fionuir."

"But if it is true?"

"It won't be happening tonight. If it was, Ailin would not have been hanging around the court. He would be getting ready for whatever ritual he needed to conduct to bring Fionuir back." I hoped I was right.

I heard Lionel's jaw crack in another yawn. "Okay, Quinn. I'll get some sleep. Are you going to bed?"

I shook my head. "I need to think some things over. I want to be ready when Beacon gets back. And I need some time to rest my mind."

He said goodnight and within a few minutes all I could hear was the wind blowing through the trees in my backyard and a coyote yipping a couple of blocks away.

I had no clue what to do.

CHAPTER 16

I finally gave up trying to find a solution to all my problems around two in the morning and went to sleep. I had hoped that Beacon would have come back before I went to bed, but there was no sign of him. Now it was mid-morning. The sun was warm, and I was sitting in my backyard sipping some strong sweet tea, preparing myself for some meditation and waiting for Lionel to return from grocery shopping.

"Quinn Larson," the voice was harsh, and yet somehow, seductive.

"Good morning, Morrigan." I tensed. Without my sight, I wouldn't be able to duck if she decided to attack. "What can I do for you today?"

"You can do nothing for me, wizard," she murmured, the harshness gone from her voice. "I do not need anything. I take what I want."

One thing about being blind, it made me immune to her seduction. "Have you come to take me?"

I heard a ruffle of feathers and then the harsh voice of the crow came through. "No, it is not your time."

"I have been seeing you a lot lately, well so to speak." One did not directly ask beings of her rank what they were up to.

"Yes," she cawed. "It is annoying that you cannot see me."

If that was the case, maybe she could make a change. "I would prefer to see you. Is it possible you can change my situation?"

"No. I cannot do anything to help in that. Healing is not what I do."

I should have thought that through. "Then how can I help you?"

"I see a power around you, wizard. I am curious what that power will do."

I felt her alight on my knee, lighter than a person but heavier than a crow. I trusted that I would survive the touch. My knee suddenly became warm. Her weight increased, and I didn't need my eyes to know I had a woman on my lap. Apparently, she'd given some thought to how to use her sexuality on a blind man. I struggled not to react and had some success but couldn't quite think straight. I thought about ice cubes and cold showers. "Does this mean you will be appearing to my apprentice and friends more often?"

"Yes. Your lovely apprentice. He blushes so easily. You might teach him some restraint." A warm laugh tickled my libido. "Or perhaps you should give him the opportunity to learn some of the more, shall we say, exotic forms of magic casting."

I didn't want to imagine the mess that Lionel would make of a spell based on sexual energy. "Perhaps when he's grasped the more basic magic." I'd had enough of this play. Maybe she had something that would help. "Do you know what I am dealing with at the moment?"

Her weight shifted back toward the bird scale. "It is boring to play with you, Quinn. Yes, I know what you are dealing with. I am not in a position to help you."

"It would help to know which side you support." I was stepping very close to the edge of not showing the proper respect, but I figured I was still on the right side of the line.

"I am on the side of The Morrigan, as I always am, Quinn Larson." She hopped off my knee.

"Thank you. I hope we will not find ourselves at cross purposes."

A ripple of her laugher warmed my soul again.

"I am sure we will at some point. Do not fret, in both your current circumstances, I am not against you. But there is a darkness in your future."

I suddenly felt the heat of the sun again. The Morrigan's warmth had covered the fact that her presence brought with it the chill of death.

I went back into the kitchen; my tea was cold and so were my bones. The Morrigan might not have been there for my death, but every time we got that close, I felt myself slide an inch closer to the grave. I hoped that didn't mean she was taking me piece by piece. If that darkness she saw was my death, I didn't want to anticipate it.

I felt around in the cupboard, but only found what smelled like chamomile tea. I didn't need to nap. I needed some stimulation. I'd have to wait for Lionel to come back for that.

Just as I finished the thought, the door opened. I heard Lionel say, "Wait here."

I heard him place bags on the counter. "What's going on?"

"Can I invite Sting and Burr in? They have some news." He sounded uncertain.

"Lionel, you don't have to ask permission. I didn't invite you to live in one of the spare rooms for nothing; this is your home too. If you are worried, just invite for a single visit."

"I just don't like to take the risk. What if I miss something?"

I despaired of him becoming more confident. "Don't worry so much. You can't invite people to the work room, and anyone you accidentally invite up here can only do minimal damage. Now go invite them in before they get distracted."

The reason I couldn't do the invitation was that you needed to be able to see who you were inviting in. That way they couldn't sneak someone in without you noticing. There were very few Real Folk who could resist the opportunity to have access to a wizard's home.

"Quinn Larson," Burr's squeaky voice called. "We have news for you. We saw someone take treasure. We saw a sidhe. It was a —" she was so excited her voice rose into the 'only dogs can hear it' range.

I patted the stool beside me. "Sit for a moment and tell me exactly what you saw. But slowly."

I heard a buzz of wings as she made her way to the seat. "Come on, Sting," Burr said. "There's plenty of room."

When they were settled, I asked them to start from the top.

"We were walking in the park, we wanted to see these new people," Burr started.

"The synymphs," Sting clarified.

"Yes, he knows." Burr made a shushing sound. "We wanted to know if they were going to be friend or enemy."

"Or maybe both," Sting interrupted again.

"That's fairy business, Sting. Be quiet and let me tell this story."

I tried not to laugh. Their information was vital and I wished there was some way to speed up the process, but if I tried, there would be something missing. Even when I was on their side, the fairies couldn't help their secretive nature.

"Anyway, there was only the old man synymph there. He was very nice to talk to, but hard to understand. He said things differently and some words I had never heard before. It is interesting that we don't understand each other." She paused as though it was a question.

"They come from very far away," I said.

"Yes. Anyway, he said his daughters were exploring the world and we should come back later if we wanted to talk to them. And he said they only wanted to live peacefully in their new land. So, I guess they were planning to be friends."

She took a breath and I suppressed the urge to hurry her along. Lionel was busy making tea, so I didn't have to worry he would interrupt.

"So, then we left," Sting prompted. "Tell them what happened when we left."

"I'm getting to that."

"Well, get to it."

I had to agree with Sting.

Burr sighed and I could imagine her eyes rolling. "So, then we left. And we decided to go through the rose garden and visit a few of our friends. And that meant we had to go through the dankness. You know where that is?"

"No, I've never heard of it." I felt safe answering the question because it couldn't distract from the story.

"I know it," Lionel said. "It's between Beaver Lake and the synymph's area. I don't know that I would say it was on the way to the entrance."

I held my breath. Would Burr get distracted?

"It is on the way, but you don't have to know why." Burr was clearly miffed.

"Please, tell us the rest of the story." I tried to sound encouraging.

"Yes, so we were trying to avoid getting wet, it makes you stink for days. And we saw something move in the center of the dankness. I told Sting to stop."

"No, I told you to stop. I was the one who saw the sidhe."

"It doesn't matter, Sting. Let me tell the story."

I heard Sting mutter something, but he kept it very quiet.

"Anyway," Burr continued. "We saw this sidhe in the middle of the dankness. She had a box and there was a hole in the ground.

She tipped the box and out came some of the treasure. It was Pansy treasure."

She? "Can you take us there?"

"Yes, but not until tonight. Too many humans. Will you get our treasure back?" Burr sounded as if she was about to cry.

"And our babies?" Sting added.

"We'll go check it out and come back with a plan. Meet us in the rose garden tomorrow at sundown."

BY THE TIME LIONEL AND I HAD EATEN LUNCH, I WAS GETTING worried about Beacon. I had hoped he would be back before sunrise, but knew it was a bit ambitious. Now that he'd been out among humans for almost a day, I could feel the little niggling doubts. Had we done a good job on the glamour? I know Lionel cast it, but it was my responsibility to make sure the right spell was cast.

Were the ingredients fresh enough? I couldn't remember when we'd trimmed the mint.

Would it have been smarter to send Lionel to follow the girl? He was more her age than Beacon and wouldn't be so conspicuous. And we wouldn't need a glamour – something that can fail – just a change of clothes.

What would I do if he was caught? What would Moss do to me? And, what was more frightening to contemplate, what would the humans do?

"What's wrong, Quinn? You look like you've swallowed a bitter plum," Lionel's voice broke my anxiety spiral.

I guess I need to think more about my expression. "I think we might need to go out and find Beacon."

"He might have had some trouble finding the girl," Lionel said. "But the glamour would have held if he was seen."

I didn't want to undermine his confidence in his spell. "You're right. I am probably worrying over nothing. Even if he was discovered, the glamour will hold for a week before it fades."

He grunted and then said, "Sure, in a week we could find him and fix whatever is wrong."

Lionel suffered from the same species' blindness that other young wizards did. Because they mostly stuck to wizardly pursuits, and we looked like humans, they didn't understand how the other species were so different. By the time Lionel passed his hundredth birthday, he'd realize that he could only pass for human as long as he didn't make friends with them. Friends are people who might ask questions about how well he was aging.

Lionel cleared his throat before saying, "Uh, Quinn, what would be so bad if the humans found out about us? I mean they found the vampires and it didn't affect any of us."

"We were lucky. And it did affect some of us. I had vampire friends who were killed."

"Sorry, I guess I meant we survived."

"Yes, we did. But the vampires were not the only Real Folk to feel the pain of human fear. They still talk about the witch trials. The humans have decided it was some kind of hysteria that was kicked off by some wheat mold. But it really did start with them finding a witch. In the end, they were burning women who didn't keep their place, but it started with real witches. We lost a hundred family lines in that one."

"Oh, I didn't know it was that bad," Lionel said quietly.

"I know. We don't talk about it. When you finish your apprenticeship, you'll learn many facts that we only share with full wizards." I realized this was not a good path for us to go down right now. "Don't worry, Beacon will be fine."

"You don't think the humans have changed? I mean, will there be a time when we can live openly together?"

Lionel sounded so hopeful I hated to tell him what I really thought. "Maybe one day, in our lifetimes, but not today. I'm sure the humans will happily stop killing each other if we give them a new target." I sighed. "If we're going to look for Beacon, we should go now. I want to go check out the park tonight before we meet Burr and Sting tomorrow."

"I was wondering if we should go look. I don't mean to say Burr and Sting won't show up or anything, but I'd like to know more about where we're going before they lead us there."

Lionel was getting smarter. "You know how to get us there right?"

He laughed. "Yes, not a problem. Dirant and I had a long conversation about the relative merits of the dankness. The wood imps find it refreshing. I found it more likely to gag me than refresh me. And, now I think about it, that stink at the sidhe court could have been from there. The cloves kind of distracted me."

"You think they use it like a spa? Wood imps lounging in the dank pools getting healthy?" The image was worth a laugh and lightened the mood. "Before we head out, let's make repellent charms. We'll push away mosquitoes and dank odors. I don't really want to resort to Ailin's overly perfumed solution to hide the smell."

Since Lionel had not tried this kind of magic before, I let him watch as I placed the charm on a teardrop shaped slip of Arbutus skin. He copied me after, and it sounded like he did it correctly. I gave him the charm I had made and took his. "Weave it into the fabric of your sweater," I suggested as I slid mine into a hidden pocket. "You don't want to drop it."

We headed for the park just as the sun was setting. I'd become skilled at assessing the time of day by the sound of the human activity. Morning was a rush and scurry noise. Midday a hungry chatter and evening a slower homeward winding down. Night was more difficult because the noise changed with the day. When I got my sight back, I hoped I would keep this sense of sound.

CHAPTER 17

When we got to the park, there were humans around, going for pre-dinner walks. In the spring and summer, they would be setting up picnics, but at this time of year they were pretty much guaranteed to be gone within the next hour.

"There's no one looking. We're going to just step into the trees." Lionel gave a slight tug to my right arm. "Be careful. It's a bit rough."

I almost went down on my knees as I stumbled over a fallen tree. "I need a bit more information, Lionel. In fact, don't worry about over guiding me."

He touched my elbow before saying, "It's better a few feet in. Right now, you have a dip in the path and four tree roots to step over. When we get past that, just follow my lead and I'll take you through a smooth track between the trees."

I shuffled my way along with my hand on his shoulder until he paused to say, "We're on a smoother track."

"Just don't go too fast," I requested.

"You'll smell the dankness soon," he said. "Wait, unless the spell will stop us smelling it?"

I concentrated on following his movements. The path was smooth, but not straight. We were moving in a zig zag – or more accurately a zig zig zag zig – path. "No, it shouldn't affect anything about us. We'll hear the mosquitoes and smell the dankness. Is it far?"

"Not too far. We're skirting the edge of the lake right now." I heard him sniff. "It's close, can you smell it?"

I could, a little moldy and a lot wet.

Lionel came to a stop. Not so abruptly that I banged into him, but enough that I knew not to speak until he did. "There's someone there," he breathed into my ear. "A female sidhe."

What was a female sidhe doing in the forest? They usually preferred the luxury of court. "Do you recognizer her?" I asked in a similar whisper.

"I saw her at court, but I don't know who she is." Lionel shifted to the side as he spoke, and then went still under my touch. I waited, knowing he'd speak when it was safe.

"One of the twins is with her."

"Okay, can we follow them?" The twin being here was a confirmation that they were involved with whatever Ailin was planning. They had been pets for Fionuir, so they would love to see her back. But it was worrying me that we had two unknown sidhe involved. I needed to know how many of them were plotting against Maeve.

"Yes, we're far enough away that they probably won't know we're here as long as we keep quiet." He started forward.

I pressed my lips together hoping it would work to keep me from making noise if I stumbled. We trailed along for ten minutes without comment. I felt trees as I brushed past them, but didn't hear any other Real Folk, including the sidhe.

When Lionel stopped again, I heard him gasp. "What?" I asked.

He tapped my hand. "It's another sidhe. We're on the edge of the dankness, don't step forward or you'll go in up to your knees. Listen."

I pushed all noise from my consciousness. Then I heard words coming from ahead.

"How much more do we need, Ailin?" It was Owen.

"It will be a few more days, I think. You can't take too much more than you have without someone seeing you. We can't be found out now. We're too close."

"When will you need us?" The woman asked.

I held myself still. If we could find out when, it would be so much easier to stop them.

"It will be – what was that?"

A shower of leaves and pinecones fell from a tree that was between us and the sidhe.

"It was nothing. Animals disturbing the trees," Owen said.

"I don't care if it was animals," Ailin snapped. Then his voice dropped. "We shouldn't talk here. You don't know who is listening. The forest Folk are sneaky and gossipy, and that spell doesn't seem to be keeping them out as much as I want. Go and we'll discuss this later."

I heard a slither of coins and then nothing. I trusted Lionel to tell me when it was safe to talk, but it was difficult to not to ask what was going on. After what felt like an age, but was probably only one or two minutes, Lionel said, "They are gone. I don't know if we learned anything useful."

"Is Ailin gone too?"

Lionel said that he was.

"We learned a lot. Can we get to where they were standing? It's the stash of fairy treasure."

Lionel started forwards and I heard a sucking noise. He pushed back at my hand. "Don't come. It's not safe. Um, can you give me a pull?"

I stepped back and braced myself, Lionel came out of the muck with a jerk.

"Thanks," he said, his voice strained. "Will you wait here while I find the path?"

"How will you get out if you step into more quicksand?" I gestured for him to move forward. "We'll take it slow."

I followed as closely as I could, trying to keep myself centered behind him. I could tell he was testing each step. It might take us a long time to get there, but we'd get there.

"It will be easier getting out. I watched where the sidhe stepped."

We made it through whatever the dankness was without much mishap. When we came to a stop, Lionel said, "It's a kind of hut."

I tried to picture a hut in the middle of this muck. "We heard the coins pouring into whatever they are using as storage. This can't be too big a hut."

Lionel stepped forward and told me what he saw.

"It's not a hut after all. It's a kind of cover to a hole. There's a ladder, but I don't know if you should go down."

I didn't want to try it either. If I fell into a pit of treasure, Lionel would have to come in and get me, leaving no one to keep watch. We just needed to know what it looked like, so I said, "Cast a light down and tell me what you see."

I heard him mumble the words to a spell and then gasp. "Oh, it's full of jewels and coins. And there's something else. A lot of cocoons. But no babies."

"The cocoons are the babies. They need to be catalyzed. How much treasure is there?"

"I don't know how deep the well is, but it's too much for us to carry away. We'll need a lot of help." His voice was muffled, and I hoped he was holding onto something solid.

"Okay, dim the light. I don't want anyone seeing it. Let's figure this out." I stepped backward, careful to stay in the center of the path.

Lionel stepped back to touch my hand. "Let's get somewhere safe and dry. I could use a cup of tea."

We walked back to the edge of the trees without talking. Lionel moved a bit faster on the way out since we'd been through and I knew the path was clear.

"Over the roots, and we're back in human territory." Lionel put a hand on my arm to stop me. "Let me just check that it's clear."

He came back quickly, and I stepped out behind him without tripping again.

"Quinn, how are we going to get that treasure back to the fairies? I felt the power in that place and it's immense. It makes me think the druids were telling the truth. They are almost ready to try to bring Fionuir back."

"I know. Maybe we should have taken as much as we could carry to slow them down a bit," I said. "But then they'd know someone had found the stash."

"Do you think they will cast the spell there? I can't see Fionuir being too happy about coming back to a place like the dankness." He chuckled and I couldn't help joining in when I pictured Fionuir, ex-queen of the sidhe, picking her way across the mud path.

"They won't be able to move the treasure easily. My guess is they'll send her somewhere and have people waiting to greet her." I hoped they wouldn't pull her out of the dimensional fold in my bathroom. That's where I sent her in from, but the fold wasn't really tied to this reality.

"Will the fairies help? I mean will they help move the treasure for all of them?" Lionel asked.

He had a point. Fairies could be selfish. I didn't want to have to deal with every fairy in the area, but maybe we could get someone to lead them.

"We can ask Princess to gather enough fairies. That reminds me, we'll also have to let Burr and Sting know that the plans have changed." I hoped Beacon had been as successful as we had. We were probably going to be done with the fairies by tomorrow at this time. I was looking forward to getting back to finding out what was happening with that human girl.

CHAPTER 18

"The bowl is clean," Lionel said. "I swear I've cleaned it three times and there's no residue."

"Let me feel it." I reached out my hand. I got nervous every time Lionel prepared to do a calling spell. Even though it was different from a summoning in that there was no compulsion to obey, he'd done a few really odd summonings because of carelessness. I ran my finger around the inside of the bowl and then tried to sense any magical residue. He was right. It was clean. "Okay, go wash out my fingerprints and we'll get started."

I sent my senses out to the house wards to make sure they would contain anything that went wrong. They were solid. I gave them a touch more power. If Princess answered the call, she'd still need permission to enter. But if Beacon came back, he'd be able to get in with no problem. If he came back. If he was still out there tomorrow night, we'd go looking for him. I didn't care that the glamour would still be in place. Not checking in for two whole days was a bad sign.

Lionel came back in the room and we talked about the

components of the spell. "Just call Princess. She can come right away, and she'll be able to get the word out faster than we can."

"But if we call Burr and Sting too, they can start leading Folk there, and we will be done faster." Lionel had been arguing this point since we'd arrived home.

"No, Lionel. If you didn't have to do it alone, it's a good idea. But I can't see if you make a mistake. What if you call all the fairies in the area? If they thought they could get their treasure back, they'd all come. Imagine the sight of a thousand fairies sitting in our yard."

He sighed. "Okay, I guess you're right. Let's get this done and we can have something to eat while we wait for Princess to arrive."

I listened carefully to him pronounce the words over the spells. He made no mistakes, and I tried not to think about what he was doing that I couldn't see.

"It's done."

I asked him to clear the workroom of the residue. He talked me through the process and when he was done, the air of the room felt clear of the smoke and power of the spells. If nothing, he was a great cleaner.

We went back upstairs to wait.

"I could have put out a seeker on Beacon," Lionel offered. "At least we would know where he was."

"I know and before we go looking for him, I'll help you with that. But we need to focus on one fight at a time. I know you think that I just want to put the fairy problem behind me, but—" If I thought the fairy problem would wait another day, I'd be looking for Beacon. But it wasn't going to wait.

"It's really dangerous. I get it." He banged a mug down and a splash of tea hit my hand. "I'm sorry."

I wiped the liquid on the side of my jeans. "Don't worry. Listen to me for a minute with an open mind. The fairies can be a pain, but if it was just them, I'd put them on the back burner. They don't seem too worried about the babies, and they can always find a way to get more treasure. It is the sidhe I'm worried about."

"If Fionuir gets free, she'll cause problems for Maeve. And she'll be mad at you for putting her in the fold." He said it as though he was asking a question.

"An open mind, remember." I waited for him to agree and then continued. "Fionuir put me under an obligation. If she thinks I brought her harm, she'd own me. If Ailin decides to take us out of the equation, we'll be gone. We've been lucky up to now. If we go after the girl and the sidhe attack, we take her down too."

"If she got Cate killed, that wouldn't be bad." The fury in Lionel's voice gave me a chill.

"That's a big if. I want revenge too. But it has to be right. We have to know we have the culprit, and we have to be careful how we exact revenge."

"You can't do it. Let me. I'm an air wizard so I have fewer restrictions." He sounded way too eager to do harm.

"And far fewer options because of it. Don't rush into it. I promise we'll get what we need out of this. I promise they won't get away because of my oaths."

I heard him start to answer and I held up a hand. "I don't want to hear it, Lionel. Trust me. It's going to work out if we make sure we think it through."

This time his sigh had a shudder to it. I hoped it was his anger sliding out on that breath. We needed calm now. In a quiet voice, he said, "I trust you. It just makes me furious."

The doorbell rang and Lionel went to invite Princess into the living room.

"Why did you call me with a spell, Quinn Larson? I gave you the acorn."

I wasn't going to tell her I wanted the acorn so that I had a way to call her easily in the future. "Lionel needs practice with his spells," I said. "Tell her what we saw."

When he finished, she squealed. "Let us go now! I can bring many hands to carry away the treasure and babies. Come, Quinn Larson. Now!"

"We are going now. How will you gather others?" I felt like I was trying to slow everyone down. "I want to make sure we get in and out as quickly as possible."

"I cannot tell you about fairy lore, Quinn Larson. But I have a charm that will call the other fairies to me. We have been planning this since we noticed the loss. We will put aside our rivalries until this is done."

Princess was sounding less like a fairy and more like a general. I'd never seen fairies when they felt they were under attack, but I'd heard they were formidable. "We only go to get the babies and treasure back. Let us handle the sidhe."

She laughed. It was an ugly sound. "Unless they bring us into the fight, we will ignore the sidhe for now. But if they have done this thing, we will have satisfaction."

I shivered at the malice in her voice. "Maeve will decide what to do. I think you will have satisfaction and more."

"We will see," she said. "How do you intend to prove to the Queen that one of her subjects is betraying her?"

I was amazed at the bile in her words. I was going to ask Lionel to describe how she looked. I got the distinct feeling that the delicate fairy had disappeared, and she was more substantial, bigger.

"The sidhe who took the treasure will have left traces of their power. I am hoping that you will allow me to take enough to give as proof."

"I cannot speak for the others, but you may have a sufficient amount of my treasure. But you may not have any of my babies," she proclaimed.

Well, that was a change. The babies were finally taking some kind of precedence over the treasure. Since I'd lost my sight, and Cate, in solving the problem that allowed the fairies to have babies, I preferred it that way.

CHAPTER 19

As we made our way down the, now familiar, track, I heard little rustling noises and whispers as the fairies joined us. To me, it sounded like a legion of tiny warriors surrounded us and I worried that we would raise too much interest.

"Lionel, tell me what you can see." I kept my voice low.

"There are hundreds of fairies," he said, his voice filled with awe. "They are still joining us."

"Can you see anyone from the forest?"

"Do not fret, Quinn Larson. We have permission to enter and take back what is ours." Princess' voice cut across my worry.

"We're at the edge," Lionel said. "And Moss just joined us, so I think it's okay."

I took control of the situation. "Let's get the fairies going first. Then take me to Moss. If he has a problem with me about Beacon, I don't want it to get in the way of the treasure rescue."

I heard Lionel direct Princess to the hut and waited for him to take me to Moss.

"We will deal with this, wizard," Princess said. "You Pansies, get into the hole and start passing up treasure. We'll sort it when it's up."

And with that I lost the position of control. She continued to order fairies around. They'd probably be done and gone within half an hour. Good, the less time it took, the less likelihood that someone would find out.

Lionel touched my elbow and I started walking. The path was there, but under a few inches of stinking mud. I would need new boots and clothes after we were done.

"Quinn," Moss's voice rumbled. "If I had known that you wanted to clear this gold from my forest, I would have done it for you."

Moss was famous for his offers of help when you didn't need it any longer. "I appreciate that, Moss. But I think the fairy folk have it under control. They'll be gone soon." I could hear the tinkle of coins as they fell into sacks.

"Good. Their chatter gives me a headache," he rumbled. "Now, what have you done with my grandson?"

I couldn't lie to Moss. It wasn't a moral thing; it was just he could always tell. "He's on an errand. I expect to see him soon." Not exactly a lie. As long as he didn't ask for details, I was okay.

"I see." The words were weighted with blame. Or maybe I did that. "I came to tell you that the item you have requested is on its way."

It was good that he didn't name the amulet in front of the fairies. They might have started plotting to obtain it before we could get it back to the druids. "Thank you. I'll tell Beacon to check in with you as soon as I see him."

The rumbling voice came from farther away this time. "Be sure you do."

I felt Lionel turn under my hand. "Where now?" he asked.

"Let's get back to Princess before she forgets to give us some evidence." We struggled back through the ooze. I could still hear the activity, but it was less chatting and more grunting. The fairies must almost be done.

"There you are, wizard," Princess said. "We only need a few more trips and the pit will be empty."

"Will you be able to carry it all out?" Lionel asked. "How much can each fairy manage?"

"Do not worry. We have enough for each clan to reclaim their share."

"There seems to be a lot of Rose fairies," Lionel said suspiciously.

"We have the most treasure." She paused. "And we have assessed a tax on the other clans. After all, I was the one to use my favor up to get you to help."

"So, that means we are done?" I crossed my fingers and said a prayer.

"For now, Quinn Larson. For now. We will put guards on our treasure. I'm sure we will not have to worry about this again."

There was a sudden hush before I could respond. "Ailin," Lionel hissed. "He's coming across the forest. I think he's seen us."

I swallowed the comment I was planning to make and said, "Princess, can you be done in a few minutes?"

"No, please make sure he doesn't take back our property. There are babies hatching now. They are in danger." Her voice was filled with tears.

"Just keep working and leave this to us." I gave Lionel a little push. "Move us between the fairies and Ailin."

"Come on." He gave me a tug and I started moving. "Um, Quinn. Ailin isn't alone. There are three other sidhe with him. We're kind of outnumbered here."

I patted his shoulder and tried to convey confidence I didn't feel. "Are they coming for us, or for the fairies?"

"They've split up. Ailin and two of the others are headed to us.

One of them is going straight to the fairies, but they are already starting to disperse. They're stuffing treasure and cocoons into sacks and running. I don't think we're going to get evidence from Princess."

I shrugged. "Let's worry about that after we get out of here ourselves. Tell me what's going on."

"They are almost on us. Ailin just waved to the third sidhe to join them. I guess he's given up on the treasure." He took a long breath before continuing. "They've stopped about six feet away. We have water on both sides. I think you can take two steps to the right before you lose the path. It goes straight for about three feet, and then jogs to the left."

I created a picture in my mind and held it there as I shouted, "Ailin, you should just go back."

He laughed. "This time, wizard, you will not survive the encounter."

"So, I understand you've brought reinforcements. You must be afraid of us." The more I could delay the first attack, the more fairies would escape. I hoped if he realized he wasn't getting the treasure back, he'd go home and wait until a more pleasant venue could be found for our fight.

"Funny, Quinn. I don't know why you think I need help. You are a blind wizard who got lucky. Luck will not always find you. But, perhaps, you are counting on the skills of your apprentice." He laughed again and it was an evil sound.

I heard a murmur from the other sidhe and told myself it was fear on their part. Ignoring the crack about Lionel, I said, "It's hard to believe anyone would find luck here. I think it's more likely someone will get a face full of mud if they make a misstep." I took a slight step to the right, trying to pretend I could see. You never know, it might just put him off enough to make him go home. I told myself that's all I wanted.

"You may have saved the fairies the trouble of getting more treasure, but they are not staying to support you. All I have to deal with is you and your clumsy apprentice. Are you prepared to duel?"

A duel was a good way to end things. Dead wasn't required, but it did sometimes happen. Usually one of the combatants wasn't blind, but both were always untrustworthy. "A duel sounds like a good idea." I wanted to keep him here, now it was to my benefit. If Ailin cheated there were too many witnesses for him to get away with it. "Lionel, can you ask the fairies to stand watch? I would hate for anyone to stumble into a fight."

Ailin laughed. "We will duel elsewhere. I would not have you claim we were unfair to you."

"Don't worry. I think the sooner the better." I wasn't going to let him isolate me from any witnesses. "You'll want to get back to your scheme to rescue Fionuir."

I heard a hiss from in front of me. "What makes you think that is what I'm doing?"

"Do you really think it's a secret? I heard it from the druids. If they know, then it's pretty much common knowledge. It won't be long before Maeve learns."

"She won't hear about it. Maeve keeps herself surrounded by people who protect her from reality. She will learn the truth when I escort the true queen back into the court."

The arrogant twit. He thought Fionuir would thank him for bringing her back. If I knew her, she'd start by punishing him for taking so long.

"And then what?" I asked, because my curiosity was tickled. Lionel had squished away when I asked for witnesses, now he sloshed back to tell us twelve fairies were coming.

I heard a slurry of whispering and then Ailin said, "If you want to go, then go, but do not expect to be rewarded for almost helping."

"Losing support, Ailin?" I called.

"No, fool. I need no support."

"Perhaps, but you didn't answer my question. What then, when you have Fionuir back?"

"I will reinstall her as queen, and Maeve will return to her studies. We need leadership not lessons. Now, are you ready to begin the duel? Your witnesses are in place."

I started to say yes as I shifted a protection charm into my hand, but a voice came from behind me. "There will be no duel."

"Maeve," Lionel whispered her name. "She is here with what looks like half the court. Perhaps we should step aside."

I followed his lead and stepped to what I thought was the edge of the path.

"She'll pass very close. Try not to lean forward and you won't touch her."

I sucked myself into as tall and thin a line as possible. I didn't need to get in trouble with the sidhe queen just as I'm getting out of trouble with the sidhe rebels. I felt a breeze of clean air slide by and I relaxed. It was time to listen and enjoy the show. Then my mouth betrayed me. "Maeve, this is my fight. I mean..."

"I know what you mean wizard," her voice was sharp. "I disagree. This fool has disobeyed me. He is attempting treason."

I realized I didn't care about treason. That was a sidhe problem. Fionuir deserved to stay in the fold because of Cate. If she hadn't been causing problems, Cate wouldn't have been in the doorway when the demon came hunting. "He's trying to bring back Fionuir. I can't let that happen."

I felt her presence next to me and resisted the urge to step back. "I will ensure it does not happen. I do not wish to make you step aside, but I will not allow you to come between me and my rights as Queen."

My stomach turned. I tried to talk, but the words stayed in my throat. She was using a compulsion on me and I had no counter-spell. All I had was my will. If I pushed it, I wouldn't win and Ailin would get his chance to run. But I didn't want to just let her decide his fate. "Are you sure you will put an end to it?"

I felt her move away and heard her soft chuckle. "Do not worry, wizard. I will make the punishment fit."

A cough came from the direction I remember Ailin standing. "I don't know what you have heard, Maeve, but there is nothing for you to concern yourself with. This is between me and the wizard."

"Your own words condemn you, Ailin. I have been watching you for some time. You realize it was a mistake to bring Owen and Garnet into your little rebellion. They may be pretty enough to guard the door, but they have less than a thought between themselves."

Point to Maeve.

"I don't—" Ailin hesitated.

"I know you don't. But you were preparing to duel with Quinn. Now you will face me," Maeve said. I heard a rustle of cloth and suddenly the fresh air surrounded me again. "I think you deserve to watch this, Quinn."

A cool cloth fell against my face. Then she whispered. "It will only work for the time it takes me to deal with this threat."

I saw everything in a black and white grainy flicker. It was headache inducing, but I ignored the pulse of pain.

CHAPTER 20

With the odd grainy sight, I could tell which parts of the ground were solid and which were simply a muddy bog. Maeve stood in the center of a circle of firm ground, Ailin across from her in a similar space. His allies were gone. We were on a thin path, but able to see both participants.

I turned my head to see Lionel, but the sight faded to black as I moved my focus away from the duel. I reached out hoping he would notice and make contact, so I knew where he was. It might come to a point where I would have to protect us, and I needed information.

He touched my hand and I told him my limitations. "The fairies are gone, all except Princess. And I can see Moss watching from behind a group of trees."

"Okay, this could get dangerous. Where is Princess, exactly?" I figured Moss could take care of himself, but I wasn't going to let Princess get hurt.

"She's coming to stand with us."

"Can you both stand in front of me and still allow me to see the fight?"

Instead of answering, Lionel and Princess appeared to the side of my vision. They were close enough for me to cover them with a protective cone.

I looked quickly at Maeve and she was drawing the limits of the duel. It wouldn't protect us if either of them cheated, but it was supposed to contain all magical effects. "This will be a good lesson for you Lionel. Be prepared for some pretty strong magic. If I think it's getting out of hand, you have to help reinforce my spell."

He opened his mouth and I could see the argument written on his face. I held up my hand and said, "I know you can do it, but there won't be time to hesitate. You will be better off just adding power to my casting. I promise you'll have plenty of time to learn what you need."

He nodded and turned back to watch the action. I touched Princess' shoulder to get her attention. "Princess, have you seen a duel before?"

She shook her head. Her eyes were round, drinking in everything that happened. I gave her the 'it's dangerous' speech and asked her to stand as close to me as possible. She took the opportunity to climb up onto my shoulder and crouch beside my ear.

"I will be safe, wizard. Do not shake me off."

"Okay, don't rip out my ear," I said as she took a firm hold on the fleshy part.

"I give you the first cast," Maeve's voice drew our attention.

First cast to Ailin was a good strategy. He'd throw as much power as he could into it and hope she was knocked out of her circle. But if it failed, he would be weak, and Maeve could end it with the second cast.

Ailin bowed and I could see his lips moving. He straightened and flung his fingers forward as though tossing a ball. The casting hit Maeve's shield and shattered into a spectacular fireworks display. Maeve staggered back a half step. And the reek of singed pond scum hit me. I started to choke before Lionel cast a spell to clear the air.

Maeve laughed and Ailin swore. The duel would be over in a few seconds unless he had some strong defensive spells.

"You are a child, Ailin. Are you prepared to die for your rebellion?"

"Kill him," Princess whispered in my ear. Personally, I hoped Maeve would be merciful. Killing Ailin wouldn't necessarily kill the rebellion. It was easy to rally people behind a martyr.

"I am prepared to die to protect my allies." He swallowed after speaking. Apparently not feeling as confident as his words would have us think.

While she was waiting for him to answer, Maeve gathered energy into a ball of blazing white in her hand. She tossed it up and down as though testing its weight. "Honorable. At least you have not abandoned all that it means to be part of the court."

She looked at the energy in her hands, then spoke again, "Will you tell me who you were working with?"

Hope lit his face. "If I do, what will you do to them?"

"I do not know, but they will survive. I can promise that." Her smile might be meant to reassure, but I felt my stomach clench with fear.

Ailin wilted a little. He kept his eyes on the energy ball as he spoke, "You cannot really mean to leave Fionuir where she is forever. Are you afraid that she will unseat you?"

The smile fell from her face. "I do not fear her. It is not my place to release her. She has done damage to many others, including you." She looked at the energy blazing through her fingers. "Perhaps to me as well."

Maeve looked up at Ailin again and suddenly drew back her hand and hurled the energy at him. By the look on his face, Ailin didn't have enough power to defend against it.

He dropped to one knee and poured his own energy into a

shield. I held my breath. Princess pulled at my hair. The ball touched the shield and shattered into a legion of butterflies.

"I will not kill one of my own court, no matter how badly they have behaved. But for twelve hours, I will not protect you from others who wish to do you harm. You will have to meet your enemies while you are weakened. I hope you will survive and learn what it feels like to be the victim."

Maeve waved her hand in a graceful circle and the glow of her protections dissolved. Ailin's energy dome flickered and crackled out.

My vision was starting to fade, but I saw her turn and take a cloak from one of her courtiers before striding away. I wanted to beg her to let me keep the sight, but she was moving with purpose and I always knew I could find her.

"I will ask the twins what they know about your other rebels. I imagine they will be more willing to share information." She threw the words over her shoulder as though they were an afterthought.

The forest went silent, and then small sounds came back as my vision faded.

CHAPTER 21

Princess launched herself from my shoulder. I tried to catch her, but I was worried about hurting her in my blind grabbing. "Lionel, stop her."

By the sound of the hissing and spitting of an angry fairy, I assumed he had managed to hold her back from Ailin. "Lionel, what is going on?"

"Ooph. Just a minute, Quinn." I heard him snap something at Princess then she went quiet. "Okay, here's where we are. Ailin seems to be held in place, at least for now. We apparently are given some time to exact our punishment on him. He's not looking too happy about that."

Interesting, Maeve had depths of malice I hoped would never be aimed at me. "And Princess?"

"She has agreed to wait until we can discuss the next steps. But I believe her plan is to scratch his eyes out so the blood will attract every biting insect in the forest, and then push him into the mud." He grunted again. "Princess wants us to hurry up, and, I have to say I like her plan."

Part of me agreed with him, but Ailin wasn't the problem in the long term. Fionuir was. I couldn't get over the feeling that she was exerting some kind of influence in this world. I would have to check to see if there was any leakage on the spell. "If that is what you believe to be right, Princess, please just get me out of earshot. I will not interfere, but don't wish to hear the consequences of your actions."

A tiny hand slapped my face. "Damn you wizard. Now I must hear your ideas. You make me feel stupid for reacting."

"Come away, Princess," Lionel said. "If Quinn thinks we need to talk before we act, I suggest we take the time to listen."

I sighed. I tried to pretend that it was a wise and deep exhalation, but it was a sigh. "I didn't mean to sound judgmental. I can't hurt Ailin. It's not because of my obligation to do no harm to sidhe, nor is it all because I'm a spirit wizard. It's because I think he's going to face a more terrible punishment from the sidhe court than we can possibly mete out. If we can avoid staining ourselves with his blood, it might be better in the end. Don't forget, sidhe thrive on their standing within the court, and Ailin will have none."

"I am not willing to let others take payment for me. He stole my babies. He stole my treasure. I do not care what he wanted them for. I will have my revenge." Princess' fury rose with every word.

"I did not think of it that way," Lionel said. "I will do as you do, Quinn. But I am afraid that Princess will be hurt if she attempts to do this alone."

"Do not worry about me, wizard," she hissed at him. "I will be fine."

I could feel Ailin's power recover. It was only a slight increase but growing as we spoke. "He will be too strong for her soon. Lionel, you will have to protect her, if you don't let her go now."

"Do you think I have time to get you out of the area?" His voice was strained. "I don't know how long I can keep her from attacking."

"You do not keep me from attacking, apprentice. I am simply

listening to you because I am not a child. I can listen." The heat had gone from her words.

"Princess, he can still harm you. Please, if you need to hurt him, allow Lionel to assist." I couldn't just let Ailin hurt her without consequences. It could start a war. "Please, let him keep you from harm."

Before she could answer, I heard a scream. "Lionel? What's going on? Are you hurt?"

A lifetime passed before he answered. "It wasn't me. It was Ailin. The synymphs... they attacked him."

"And?"

"They've slashed his face. He is..."

"He is maimed for life," the glee in Princess' voice was disturbing. "I am satisfied, good night."

"One of the synymphs is coming here," Lionel whispered.

I waited, curious. The smell of the dankness cleared in a wave of eucalyptus. "Wizard." The voice was sibilant and oddly accented. "These sidhe came to us as friends when we first arrived. They told us that this hole was sacred to them and begged us leave to use it. We did not know they would put it to such terrible use. We are not accustomed to allowing others to violate our territory. We thank you for bringing this to an end. We will provide you with one boon."

The eucalyptus faded and the funk of the dankness threatened to overwhelm me. "Let's get out of here, Lionel. We are going to have to burn these clothes."

"It seems Ailin will be here alone for a while. I see Moss is back. Do you think he'll have a go at Ailin?"

I turned and started along the path I remembered before speaking. "I don't know. But we should go. I can't be responsible for every being that has a bone to pick with Ailin."

CHAPTER 22

We made it out of the park without any further problem. I hoped Ailin was able to leave soon after, but from the description, even if he could find a healer, he was likely to have a scar. Sidhe did not like disfigurement. Princess was right. No matter how long it took for him to worm his way back into a position of power, he would have a reminder that he'd made a mistake in his alliance.

Lionel led me to our front door. I had hoped to find Beacon waiting for us, but no luck.

"Let's get this stink off us. Go shower and change. Use the rosemary soap," I said. "And burn these clothes. I'll buy you some new ones."

Fifteen minutes later we were in my work room.

"I think the spell is in the blue book with the yellow spine," I said. While I was sluicing off the stench of the dankness, I'd had an idea. There was an old spell that could let you visualize the subject. "If we can see what Beacon's doing – at least if you can see – we might be able to assure Moss and buy us some time. And I might be able to stop worrying." I had that feeling we'd avoided the frying pan, but Moss was an unknown fire that was scorching my toes. Little snippets of stories of people who went missing after getting on Moss's wrong side kept popping into my mind.

I heard the book slap down on the table. And then a huge yawn erupted. "Sorry, Quinn."

I waved away his apology. "Can you flip through and find the spell?"

"Uh huh. Give me a second."

I waited. All I heard was the flipping of pages. Then the sound slowed down suddenly. "Lionel?"

"Oh, uh just a second. Here it is, and I think I can do it. We need something from Beacon. His mug is upstairs, and I don't think I washed it since he was here last. And we need an idea where he is. That should..." he yawned again. "That should work."

I gave up. He was liable to fall asleep in the middle of the spell. "Just get me the mug and read me the spell."

"No, I can do this." He yawned again. "Okay, but maybe we can do it after I've had a couple of hours' sleep."

I felt for him. I remembered that feeling of loss for every spell I didn't get to cast. But he was too tired. "You can try it when you've had enough sleep. I will cast it now, so I can stop worrying. Go get the mug."

While he was gone, I started the process of clearing my mind of everything that had happened in the last twenty-four hours. I needed to memorize the spell as he read it and figure out how to twist it a bit so it gave sound, not just sight.

"Here," Lionel pushed the mug into my hand. "Let me read it through first."

Again, I waited.

"Okay, here's how it works. You use the mug as a platform for the spell. I guess that might be hard on some things, like a hair for example."

"Lionel, the spell, please."

"Oh, yeah. Place the mug in the center of the casting circle. Throw your power to the place you last saw the subject and say the name of the spirit who protects the subject, while thinking what you want to know."

"Okay, draw the circle around me and go. I'll sleep in the circle if need be."

He sealed me in, and I couldn't hear anything else. I reached for the mug and kept the fingers of my right hand on the edge so I wouldn't lose track of it when I started with the spell.

The last place I'd seen— well known he was there— Beacon was upstairs. I assume the spell would trace him from there. I sent a thread of power up and said the name of Beacon's protective spirit. It was a good safeguard. Only friends knew that information, so no one could snoop on just anyone.

I felt a slight tug at the power thread and sat back to wait for results.

Sounds of traffic came through, then words flashed by, garbled, and I realize I was hearing time pass as well as distance.

A long few minutes passed with silence and I started to think I'd done something wrong when I heard giggling.

"Okay, see ya later." A girl's voice called out. "Are you sure you don't need a ride home?"

"No, you know it's only a couple of blocks away, that's why we hang out here." The other voice belonged to our mystery girl.

I heard footsteps walking away, and then the sound of a second set of footsteps following closely: Beacon.

Had he found her at the club? If so, why was he taking so long? I heard a cat singing to his mate, a car horn and then the first set of footsteps sped up. A gate creaked, a door slammed, and then silence.

After a second, I heard a thunk; Beacon's toolbox dropping. Then a rustle of leaves and a long sigh. He was settling in for the night.

I wouldn't get anything else from the spell unless Beacon

started to narrate his observations. I pulled the thread of power back to me and prepared to curl up on the bare floor until morning. I reached behind me to feel for the edge of the salt circle and my fingers brushed something soft. Lionel had left a blanket inside the circle with me.

CHAPTER 23

Despite the blanket I was chilled when Lionel came down in the early morning to clear the circle.

"There were a couple of loose spirits," he said. "Don't worry they're gone. Come up and get some breakfast while you tell me what you learned."

I groaned at the stiffness in my bones as I straightened. "I didn't get much. He's still okay, and I think he's within a couple of blocks of the bar we went to that night."

"Here, have some tea while I heat up the oatmeal." Lionel put a mug into my hand. "Maybe you should get a couple of hours more sleep before we go looking."

"No, I think we should go as soon as I get washed and changed. It's early enough that we should be able to avoid a lot of humans."

"If you are sure, then eat this," he said. I heard the scrape of a bowl on the countertop. "We can be on our way as soon as you are done."

I washed the oatmeal down with the last of the tea and was about to ask Lionel for my coat when someone knocked at the door. Please, don't let it be a fairy asking for a favor.

"I'll go see who it is," Lionel said, passing me my coat.

"Oh, hi. You can come into the hall. Quinn, you had better come."

I felt my way toward him.

"It's a—"

"I am a pea sprite, Solen is the name," a voice squeaked out. "Pleased to meet you and all that, but I have to give you this and get on my way. Too many eyes here."

"I'll take it," Lionel said.

"No, I can only hand this to Quinn Larson."

I held out my hand.

"Lower you fool, do you expect me to jump? Oh, I forgot. They told me you were blind. Must be hard. Drop your hand a foot. There you go."

I felt the weight of the Gur amulet slip into my palm. "Thank you."

"No problem. Anyway, I have to be on my way. The wife is waiting, and I don't want to be on her wrong side right now, you know what I mean. You take care."

The babbling stopped.

Lionel closed the door. "I suppose you should hide that somewhere before we go."

"Yes, and we need to be back by dark because the druids will be waiting." I hoped there wouldn't be too many druids. My neighbors might get suspicious if too many hooded men were standing outside my door for too long.

I started to go back into the kitchen. The sugar jar would hold the amulet while we were out. Before I took two steps, the door knocker rapped again. I slipped the amulet into my pocket, just in case I needed to protect it.

"Uh, Quinn," Lionel said. "It's the druids."

"Okay, invite them in. Just to the living room." I felt my way to the couch and carefully placed the amulet on the coffee table.

"I see the amulet arrived," the one I'd come to think of as the spokes-druid, or the voice anyway, I still figured it was more than one, started right in. No pleasantries.

"It just arrived. How did you know?"

"You can have the answer to that question, or I will tell you which of the pieces of information we gave you was false."

Not really a choice. "I'll take the latter."

"First, we must take the amulet."

I gestured for them to take it. Then I heard whispering before the spokes-druid said, "You have cleansed the amulet well, we thank you. The false knowledge is in regard to the human."

"What?" Lionel blurted out the question.

I patted the air to try and calm him down. "I thank you."

The druids left in a slap of sandals and Lionel rushed back.

"How could that be the false information? The girl is definitely involved."

I agreed it was not what I would have guessed. "The druids don't lie outright. But they don't always speak the full truth. Do you remember exactly what they said about her?"

I tried to bring the words out of my memory, but Lionel beat me to it.

"They said she was not what she seemed. And they said someone was protecting her, and they said she had something to do with the summoning."

"That's about what I remember. They also said she didn't know what she had done." Damn, it was never simple when druids got involved.

Lionel hummed his thinking song again and then said, "So, maybe we should just go get Beacon and look elsewhere for the culprit."

I stood up. "Let's start with finding Beacon."

It was going to take about an hour to walk to the bar, plenty of time to work through the implications with Lionel. "Look, don't be too disappointed. The thing is we have four pieces of information about her. They said the false knowledge is about her. But that could be only one of the four pieces of information. I find it really hard to believe they brought her into the equation if she wasn't important."

He stopped walking and I almost lost contact with the arm I was holding. I really had to break him of the habit of stopping like that.

"So, she might know what she did? Or someone isn't protecting her, or she really didn't have anything to do with the demon, or she is exactly what she seems?"

"Right, or it could be really subtle." I prodded him to keep walking. "Regardless, I'm not about to waste the time we've spent trying to find her. We'll keep going on the assumption that she is important. No one puts a glamour on an unimportant human."

"THIS LOOKS LIKE A NICE PLACE TO HANG OUT," LIONEL SAID AS we crossed the street to the bar where I'd seen the girl and her friends. "I mean, it's bright and the people all look kind of happy."

I remembered that it felt like a place where people went to pretend they were important, or attractive, or both. But then I might have felt different if I was Lionel's age. He was old enough to be the girl's grandfather, but he looked like he was young enough to be her friend.

"If I remember correctly, there's a house close by with a lot of shrubs where Beacon could have hidden." I figured we could set the trail spell from there and find Beacon pretty quickly. "The girl had said she lived within a couple of blocks."

When we were tucked away from sight in the shade of a rhododendron, I told Lionel to rip open the envelope containing the tracking powder. I heard the sharp rip and Lionel's whisper of "Beacon."

It usually took a few minutes for the spell to settle, when it was done, we would be able to follow it to Beacon's current location, but as it sought him, it would wander all over where Beacon had been since leaving.

"Is there something we can do to check out if she's protected? Like a spell?" Lionel kept his voice low.

"Not that I know about, but maybe Beacon has seen something. I have a feeling that we will need to talk to her. Will you be okay if you have to do it?"

"I guess so. I've never really talked to a human." There was wonder in his voice.

I chuckled. "I was thinking more about you talking to a pretty young girl. You go kind of shy around the ones we know."

"Well, I'll do what needs to be done," his words dripped with wounded pride.

I apologized and we stood in silence for a few more minutes, the sounds of traffic increasing with the minutes passing. I was getting a bit nervous that people would notice us when Lionel said, "It's set. Let's get going." His brusqueness belied his assurance that he wasn't bothered by my comment.

The trail would be clear to Lionel; it would have a faint glow that humans wouldn't notice. To them, it would look like snail tracks. We turned a couple of corners but after what must have been about four blocks, Lionel slowed.

He pulled me a little to the side. "It ends at a house in the middle of the street. I don't think we can just walk in; people would notice."

"Is there anyone around? Maybe we can slip in quickly." I could move fast if there weren't any obstacles.

"There's a couple coming down the street toward us. But I get the feeling that we're being watched from behind curtains," he said.

"Can you see Beacon?"

"He's under a tree. I don't think anyone else can see him. It's really shady."

I heard voices approaching. "Let me know when the two people pass." I fingered an illusion spell. "What are you wearing?"

"A black trench coat and jeans."

"You'll need to cast this," I handed him the oak leaf which held the spell. "When they pass, send an illusion of us walking on down the street."

He took the leaf and I heard him crush it a second later. "Done."

"Let's join Beacon quickly. The spell will last until the illusion reaches the end of the block and then fade. We will be unnoticed for a few seconds." He pulled me forward and through a gate. I felt the heat drop as we went under the canopy of an old tree.

"If you could make us disappear, why didn't you do it before we started following the trail?" Lionel asked.

"It's too dangerous. We might have bumped into someone. And, we weren't invisible. Anyone watching would have seen us, but people would have expected us to continue walking and when they saw that, we had a few seconds while they believed it."

"Hi, nice of you to join me," Beacon said. "She's in the house. You can see her through that window."

"There's three other people there," Lionel provided a narration. "Parents and it looks like a little brother."

Beacon added, "Do humans work differently? I mean shouldn't they look a bit alike?"

"The parents and the boy look similar; they all have dark hair and are kind of short. But the girl is tall and she's blond," Lionel explained.

"She said they were foster parents," I said.

"She looks happy," Lionel continued. "I don't know how we are going to get her away from them."

"We'll think of something. She's a teenager. She'll leave the house at some point. We'll find a way to talk to her." It was going to be difficult. I knew enough of human activity to know that teenage girls were always told not to talk to strangers.

"How long have you been here?" I asked Beacon.

"Since last night. It took a long time for her to show up at that bar. I didn't want to leave when they went to bed and miss her in the morning. I shouldn't have bothered. She hasn't done anything but hang out with her family since she got up."

"It looks like the disguise is working well, though," Lionel said. "You still look like a human."

"Yeah, but my skin is kind of itchy. It's like there's a film on it. Is that normal?"

I'd never heard of that effect. "When did it start?"

"A couple of hours ago."

"Lionel, can you see if he has a rash or anything?"

Lionel shifted away from my side. "No, his skin looks smooth."

I moved toward their voices. "Can I feel your skin?"

Beacon said I could and put my hand on his arm. Lionel was right. Beacon's skin was smooth like a baby. "The spell figures out how to disguise you. I guess it coated you to smooth out the bark. I'm impressed, Lionel. You set a strong spell. As soon as we get away from human eyes Lionel will remove the spell. So, what have you learned? I hope it's good stuff because Moss is kind of annoyed that you have been out of touch."

I reached out to find the trunk of the tree so I could lean against it and told Lionel to join me.

"Now that we know where she lives, do we need to stay here?" Beacon sounded plaintive. "I'm hungry and I could use a pint of Mark's finest."

We slid out of the shadows as soon as the family moved to another room.

Beacon took us back a different route than we'd taken into her neighborhood. "I like to walk on the tree-lined streets as much as I can," he said. "Some of the trees here came from seedlings in the forest. I know their mothers."

I remembered this part of town well; older houses, old trees, mature gardens. I remembered the blues and pinks of hydrangeas and the luscious colors of roses. If it wasn't so far from Stanley Park, I'd love to live here. "We'll have to cross the bridge and get close to Bank's before we can lift the disguise. Once we get into the alleys, we'll be fine."

"Yep," Beacon laughed as he spoke. "My usual homeless guy disguise is easier on the nerve endings and just as effective downtown. What the... did you see that, Lionel?"

"Yeah, is that usual?"

I was about to kick one of them. "Tell the blind wizard what you are talking about, please."

"I could have sworn I saw a Real Folk shadow," Beacon said. "Not sure what it is."

"It was short. Too short to be anything but a Real Folk," Lionel explained. "The shadow was stocky, but that doesn't mean anything. Shadows get distorted."

"Where was it?"

"In the boxwood hedge, it was running ahead of us." Lionel gave me a tug and we started moving again. "It might have been watching us. Or, it might have been visiting a neighboring garden."

"I thought they were mostly run out by the wildlife," I said.

"Not all the Folk are worried about coyotes and skunks. But it is odd to see one at this time of day." Beacon clapped me on the shoulder. "Never mind, let's get downtown so I can drop this torturous spell. My skin feels like it is going to peel."

CHAPTER 24

As soon as we could, I told Lionel to lift the spell on Beacon. His sigh of relief woke up a homeless man. Fortunately, the man was so soaked in cheap wine he didn't say anything about Beacon being far from human.

Two minutes later we were inside Banks' waiting for our beers and dinner to arrive.

"If we can get her alone," I said, "maybe we can find out what's going on. There are some spells Lionel can use to see through the protections."

Mark put the beer on the table before anyone answered.

"How do you plan to do that?" Beacon's question came out flat. "Do you imagine no one will notice a missing teenage girl?"

"We wouldn't need to keep her long enough to be missed. Maybe a couple of hours."

Lionel was quiet, which was suspicious in itself.

"Quinn, I think you are losing perspective here," Beacon continued. "Think about what will happen if she comes to harm. Or if she understands what we're doing before you have a chance to convince her you're one of the good guys."

I didn't want to think this through. The fairies had taken me away from this, and now I was ready to do what I wanted. And I wanted to know what was going on. If this girl hadn't killed Cate, she was close to who did it. "There are spells we can use to remove her memory. It wouldn't do much harm. No one would know it was us. At least, no one who would care."

"Quinn, I am not going to be part of something like that. You wouldn't let me harm Ailin, and I'm not going to let you do anything to her." Lionel jumped in. "I know you want to get your revenge. I want someone to pay for what happened to Cate, but —" I heard him slam his hand on the table. "Look, we know this girl is linked to Cate's death, but not how. Until we know who is to blame, I am not going to do anything to her."

I sat back in my chair. My mind agreed with him. In fact, my mind was appalled by what I wanted Lionel to do. But there was this small hard place inside me that didn't care. That place was occupied by all the grief and anger I'd hidden from the world when Cate died. I could keep that part of me quiet when I was busy, but without distractions, it took hold of me, and all I wanted was blood.

I rubbed my face to silence the words coming from the hard part of me. "Then what do you think we should do next? Beacon didn't follow her for that long just so we could let it go. We need to do something."

There was a loud sigh, which I assumed came from Lionel, and then nothing. I finished my beer. Lionel ordered another round. The food arrived. I picked at my dinner while I waited for them to eat. My appetite was gone, and my patience was rapidly following it.

A scrape of a bowl being pushed away signaled the end of the meal. And, before I could prompt them, Lionel said, "Maybe it would help to get Beacon's impression of her. After all, like you said, he's been following her for long enough."

I nodded, afraid to speak in case the evil part of me took over.

"Okay, it's not much. She spent time with friends and her

family. She reads a lot. I mean a lot. Any time she has five minutes, she pulls a book out of her bag. If I didn't know better, I'd think she was a druid, or a witch, she's so determined to learn."

I felt a little more rational now that we were doing something. Without these two to challenge me, I could have started something between the humans and Real Folk that I couldn't stop. Considering I'd been so worried about Fionuir starting a war, it would be stupid for me to do it.

"I didn't see anyone refresh the glamour, but I noticed it seemed to weaken a bit at the end of the day. Not so much that you'd notice if you weren't looking. Then it was fresh in the morning. You think maybe it's tied to her energy level? Like it renews itself with her essence?"

"It can be done," Lionel answered. "I seem to remember hearing about a spell that can be cast to protect someone before they go on a quest; in the old days, when a wizard had to quest at the end of his apprenticeship. But if it's been there since she was a baby, it would be stealing her essence."

Something clicked in my mind. "If she's not human, a spell that feeds off her essence would explain why she is able to live and age like a human."

"Yeah, that makes sense. The questing wizards were only going for a couple of weeks usually. The book wasn't that clear."

If he was reading the type of books that contained that spell, he probably wasn't sleeping much. "It's highly risky to do that. If she gets sick, she'll lose the glamour." I wondered if the spell was set so it would take her energy even if it risked her life.

"She seems pretty healthy," Beacon said. "I know humans get sick pretty easily sometimes, but she glows healthy."

"Did you see anything that would indicate she was capable of summoning a demon on purpose?" I had the weird feeling we were missing something. Something right in front of us.

"No, she seemed normal. She argues with her brother. She is

kind to animals, and she likes to tend the garden. I had to climb into the tree to avoid being seen when she came out to do some garden clean up. I don't think she did it on purpose, if she did it at all, Quinn."

I rolled my eyes. "So, someone used her as a conduit. They are treating her as if she were a tool. As if she had no life to herself."

"It does sound familiar," Lionel said. "But Fionuir can't be using her as a battery now. If it was her, then the spell would be fading."

"If it was Ailin, or one of his rebels, it will start fading now. They won't be going far from the court for a while." Beacon was right; maybe the girl was in danger.

There was more reason than ever to get her alone and figure out exactly what was going on. "Don't make assumptions. If Fionuir could do this, then any of the sidhe could have. In fact, there may be other Folk who could do it."

Lionel groaned. "I thought talking this through would make it more simple, not less. Is there anyone we can eliminate?"

I thought about it, and said, "Well, from everything we know, this has been going on since the girl was born, otherwise humans would have seen something was wrong. So, the synymphs are out."

"I hate to say it," Beacon said, "But Quinn's right. We need to find a way to get her alone and figure this out."

"But what about people finding out?" Lionel asked. "What about your objections?"

"If we are going to get into ethical conversations, we need more beer." Beacon called an order for another round before continuing. "It's about the why, Lionel. If we were going to do it to punish her, then we'd do it wrong. If we are trying to protect her, we'll figure out a way to do it right."

I agreed, but I only had one idea how to start. "Whatever we do, it needs to be Lionel who makes contact."

"Why? Does he have some experience in dealing with teenage human girls?" Beacon sounded amused.

"I... I don't have any experience in girls of any kind." I could hear the blush in his voice. "What do you think I might have to do?"

Beacon laughed. "Maybe you can cast a confidence spell on him. In fact, you might need to do that at some point so he can find a mate."

It was funny, but the best thing to do for Lionel was build his confidence, not keep applying spells to cover his weaknesses. "I think we'll come up with something you can handle. We just need you to bring her somewhere we can have some privacy when we talk to her. It will have to be private, but not suspicious. We want her to trust us, not run away and call the police."

"Doesn't that usually take a few dates? I mean, I can't expect her to just come somewhere with me that isn't public. And, if it's public, we can't talk to her about magic. Someone will overhear. Maybe I should ask her for coffee and then you can compel her to come to a better place, and then—"

"Calm down, Lionel." It was going to be an uphill battle to get him ready for this. "Maybe there's another way. I hate to use magic to compel her. We don't know how it will react with the protections she has."

"And the humans react oddly under compulsions, so we can't trust anything she tells us if she's under," Beacon said. "Or so I've heard."

I drank some beer and mulled it over. Beacon was being as useless as Lionel in getting a plan pulled together. I felt an urgency around this problem, as if we were running against a deadline.

"She thinks something is going on," I thought out loud. "She was dabbling in the arcane with her friends. What if Lionel met her about that? What if he said he could help them raise a ghost or something?"

"That's an idea." Lionel sounded eager all of a sudden. "Maybe

I can show them a little magic. Like that spell that raises dust spouts."

I visualized a repeat of the botched hurricane spell. "Beacon, did she go anywhere that might help Lionel get introduced?"

"Maybe. She went to a couple of places that seemed a bit odd for a human. There was a bookstore a couple of blocks from that bar. It had the same kind of Goth look as her friends; black and lace and it had old books. She spent almost an hour in there."

"Was it Rare Mystic Books?" I asked.

"Yeah, it was. Why do you know it?"

"It occasionally has real magic books. I go there every few months to see if there is anything new in." Another coincidence, maybe that's where the spell gets reinforced. I wasn't the only Real Folk who went to Rare Mystic Books.

"I could talk to her about books," Lionel said. "That would be easy as long as it's about magic."

It was looking much more likely we could succeed. Lionel would take a bit of coaching, but we might be able to talk to her within a few days.

Beacon's chair scraped. "I have to go, Quinn. If I don't go see Moss now, he'll set me some task that will tie me to the park for a week."

"Let me know if he keeps you tied up. If not, drop by the house tomorrow. I think we can work out a plan pretty quick."

"I'll try, but don't wait for me." Beacon said his goodbyes.

Lionel and I sat in silence for a while. Well, we weren't saying anything. Silence didn't exist in Banks', everyone else was chattering and laughing.

I mulled over what I'd do when we had the girl. I needed to get information. If I could get Lionel chatting with her, I could scan her. In fact, if he could get something that belonged to her we could do a deeper scan. I wouldn't let my thoughts go to what I'd do to her if she raised that demon. I tried to keep thinking we were helping her, not investigating her.

"I have an idea," Lionel's voice cut through my thoughts. "I don't think we want to wait around the store until she decides to drop by. What if we dropped a charm that would make her want to go in? We could control the time. Didn't you tell me that a charm can be tuned to a person?"

"That's a great idea. Did you see enough of her to set the spell by sight?" If we had to get something she owned it would be tricky.

"I think so. If I can't, you saw her, so you can fill in the blanks. We could do this after school, that's the day after tomorrow, right? Yes, I think we can do this." I envied his knack of seeing the possibilities.

It was time for us to go home. We had some planning to do and Lionel was going to have to learn how to talk to girls.

CHAPTER 25

Beacon had been right. He'd sent a message that Moss had set him the task of introducing the synymphs to the park Folk. He'd be there for at least a week. The good news was we'd know all about the new Folk by the time he was done. And we could do this without him.

On Monday, Lionel dropped the charm just inside Rare Mystic books, and we spent an hour going through their inventory. He found a book on herbal based spells and then we went across the street to a coffee shop to wait and read the book.

"She should be by in a few minutes," Lionel reported. "By the number of kids walking by, school just let out."

"When you talk to her, what will you say?" I'd coached him on how to approach the girl. And I hated to micromanage, but I couldn't let him bungle it.

"When she goes in, I'll follow. I'll strike up a conversation, probably about a book, or something. I'll offer to introduce her to my teacher and then I'll bring her here." He sighed. "I think I can handle it."

I got the hint and stopped asking. "If we get to talk to her, I'll take a look under the glamour. You can show her this book. It should keep her interested for a while."

"Should I tell her it's real magic in the book?" Lionel asked. He was drumming his fingers on the table, more nervous than he let on.

"It's up to you. I'll be doing the mysterious teacher thing. I'll need to touch her, so make sure you sit on the opposite side from me."

The finger drumming stopped. "She's walking past the store," Lionel said; his voice barely above a whisper. "She went right past; I don't think it worked. She just went right by. Oh, she turned back."

I smiled at his nervousness. Not that I was completely sanguine about what we were about to do. I just hid it better. "Did she go in?"

"Yes, I'm on my way."

I sat there alone. It had been a long time since I was alone in public. Blindness had made me way too dependent. It was time to take my newfound independence outside the house.

The door had a bell hanging from it to alert the barista when someone entered. After what felt like an age, the door tinkled and a gaggle of voices burst the silence. Teenagers looking for a way to seem cool. Having coffee after school was vastly better than taking drugs.

The next time the door tinkled, someone sat at my table. "Quinn, please meet Dionne Walker."

I held out my hand, Lionel must have prepared her to deal with my blindness because she didn't hesitate to take it.

"I'm delighted to meet you, my dear." I clasped her hands in mine and held on a few moments longer than necessary. The initial touch had vibrated through my bones. The protection was strong, but the touch had let me slide a probing spell beneath it. I smiled and suggested Lionel show her the book.

While they chatted, I read the probe. It showed me a strength of power that almost knocked me out of the chair. The protection didn't cover a human girl. It covered a strong witch. Somehow one of the Real Folk had ended up in foster care in a human family.

As I tried to find a clue about who she was, I heard Lionel say, "Did you even consider that you shouldn't have come with me?"

What the hell was he talking about?

"Look, you wanted me to come to the coffee shop," she responded. By the tone, this was not the first exchange of the conversation. "What could you have done? We're in the window and this is a public place. You seemed cool. You know about magic. You said your teacher might take me as a student, so I figured it was worth a risk."

"Do you take these kinds of risks often?" He pushed the point home without hearing her annoyance. What was he hoping to achieve?

"Sure, I go off with all the creepy old men who hit on me in bookstores."

I felt her shift away and was about to step in when Lionel came to his senses and said, "You're right. I was just worried about the way you just agreed to come. Please, accept my apology and stay."

She hesitated. I could feel her emotions through the probe. She was torn between a burning curiosity and annoyance at Lionel.

"Allow me to add my apologies to those of my apprentice. He sometimes gets overly protective of people." I felt the curiosity win out a split second before she settled back into the seat. It was disconcerting to feel her movements through the probe.

"Well, just remember I can take care of myself. Now, tell me more about this book."

I held up my hand, palm out, to stop Lionel answering. "Dionne, do you know what happened to your parents? I am sorry to ask so directly, but it is important."

I felt a hard knot of pain inside her. "They are dead. When I was a baby. Someone killed them and left me at a police station. Why?"

She said it like a report, but though my link I felt the raw pain that still lurked inside; pain and a feeling of betrayal. I let her pretend it didn't matter.

"It might help us understand what is happening to you," I said. "If you want me to teach you, I need to know as much as possible about your background."

I felt her withdraw physically, but the probe remained strong. It was a relief that she didn't just happily follow us wherever we led. Her suspicion meant we would have to work harder for her trust, and maybe take some risks, but I wouldn't have to feel so much like I was taking advantage.

I had no doubt that she was a witch. But she wasn't managing the glamour around her. I needed to do more tests. She would have to participate, but my guess was it was a battery. Because it was only damping her power, it would last a good long time if it was holding the life force of one of her parents.

"Lionel, is there anyone nearby?" Time to take risk one. "I think we need to give a little demonstration."

"Not here," he answered immediately. "The teenagers are paying too much attention. I think it's Dionne. She's too pretty for a teenage boy to ignore."

Dionne groaned.

It would have helped to give her a little demonstration of magic. She would find it hard to disbelieve a light ball, or a fairy image. Now I'd have to rely on the fact that teenagers always wanted to be special. They wanted to be someone else so badly that they would sometimes believe the impossible.

I let the probe go before I spoke, not wanting to take the chance that I would accidentally push a compulsion to believe through it. I needed her to trust, or not trust, on her own. "Dionne, I need to tell you something and I can't show you proof until later. I know you don't know us, but I swear we are telling you the truth."

"Look I think you are a bit weird but go ahead and tell me. I promise not to freak out." I could hear a little uncertainty in her voice, but we were just going to confirm what she already suspected, and hoped, was true if I read the emotions right.

I took a deep breath. This was a new experience. I'd never heard of a witch who didn't know exactly what she was from birth. I decided on the direct approach I didn't want her to misunderstand. "We think you are a witch. Someone who can do magic."

Silence.

Lionel took pity on me and said, "She's okay. I think."

"I am okay." Dionne's words were snapped out. "Are you serious? I can't do magic. I've never..."

"You have," I tried to keep the anger and hurt out of my voice. "You did something a few months ago. You felt something happen when you did that summoning."

"What summoning? Do you mean the séance? My friends and I found a book in Rare Mystic and it gave the steps. I wanted to talk to my mother, or my dad." Tears cracked the last words.

Her breath came in short gasps as she tried to control the tears. I heard Lionel murmuring reassurances and she seemed to calm down. We needed to get her somewhere private to help her understand what she was. And to find out who was protecting her. I was convinced someone turned her séance into a summoning. It wouldn't take much.

When her breathing was normal, I asked, "Would you come with us somewhere more private? My home has a workshop. We could show you what you can do. We could try to help you figure out where you came from."

"Could you help me find my parents? Do a real séance?"

It broke my heart to hear the hope in her voice. If I said yes, she would come wherever we asked. I couldn't say it. It was impossible to guarantee that her parents would come to speak to us, or that they were able to if they wanted. It was entirely possible they weren't both dead.

I knew, in the long run, we'd be better off earning her trust. I needed her in the long run, not just for one piece of information. "I can try. But not right away. We'll need to figure out who you are before we ask them to visit."

"Were you serious about me being a witch? Like a spell casting witch?"

"Yes," Lionel said. "You have a protection on you. We think it's in something you are carrying."

I crossed my fingers that he'd be sparing with the information. We did need to have some leverage, something we could lead her with if she needed an incentive to believe. "Lionel is right. But it's too public here for us to do our tests."

She touched my hand and I felt the probe reconnect. Her emotions were raging under a fine veneer of calm. "Will they hurt? The tests?"

I smiled. I hoped it was reassuring. "I wouldn't hurt you. The tests will relax you and you might fall asleep. At worse you'll feel dizzy."

We waited. She kept her hand on mine and I felt her shift toward agreement. She wasn't ready yet, but she was beginning to trust.

I heard people leaving. "Lionel, is it safe for you to do a small spell?"

She tensed, then removed her hand, cutting off my contact to her feelings.

"I can, but if something goes wrong..." Lionel said.

"It won't go wrong. You're fine." I ran through a list of the spells that Lionel had down pat. It had to be something that would be clearly magic, but very small. "You could call the image of someone she knows."

"How would you know who I know?" Her defenses snapped up and I gave myself a mental slap for not thinking.

"We have been looking for you. We followed you and I'm sorry, we watched you for a while. We had to know." I waited for her to react, fearing the worst.

"That's creepy. I guess if you are who you say you are, and I'm what you think I am, I can understand," she said.

Lionel cleared his throat. "I could bring her brother. I mean an image of her brother into my palm. If we crowded around and made sure no one could see."

I nodded. It would work.

"You mean you can bring Robbie here?"

"No," Lionel said. "I will show you an image, like a hologram."

"Will he know? I mean will he feel anything?" Dionne asked, fascinated. I was happy that she was asking for details, and not arguing the probability of it.

"No," I said. Lionel was not all that clear on the theory of the spells yet, so I didn't want to leave it to him to explain. "It's like taking a picture, a candid picture. He won't know it's happening because it's not happening to him."

"I guess it is okay," Dionne said.

"Okay, lean in. It will take a second." Lionel's voice was hushed.

"Can I get you anything?" The barista said, from just behind me before Lionel started speaking the first words of the spell.

"No," Dionne said, "We're good."

My heart started beating normally after a few seconds. "I think we need to go somewhere else."

CHAPTER 26

"I don't think I should go to your house." She sounded like she wanted to be convinced.

"I swear you'll be safe," Lionel said.

"Yeah, and you just gave me a lecture about going with people I don't know."

Lionel sputtered for a second and I almost stepped in to rescue him, but he needed to learn how to get himself out of situations rather than just get himself in.

"I thought maybe now you knew us enough to feel safe." His argument was really weak, and I hoped the girl was smart enough to call him on it.

Then I remembered it wasn't a game. And then I remembered she'd summoned the demon by mistake. And it didn't matter that it was a mistake. And the anger and grief started to boil. I stamped down the seething emotions. Time for them later; when we knew. "Dionne, I'm sorry, you don't know anything about us. I guess we don't know that much more about you. But what we do know makes all the difference."

"Yes, it does," she said. "I want to help you figure this out. I want to talk to my parents, and I want so much to be a witch. I just... I've just learned to be careful."

"Lionel, get us some more coffee. We can stay here a while." And another round of drinks would keep the barista away. While he was gone, I reached toward her and she took my hand. I needed to gauge how scared she was. If necessary, we could arrange for her to meet us another time, but I was anxious to get this settled today.

Lionel put mugs on the table before saying, "What do we need to do to help you feel safe?"

"Maybe some information. What do you do for a living?"

"Well I teach Lionel magic." It was going to be difficult to build her trust with the answers if her questions were going to continue along this path. "Lionel is my student."

"You don't have jobs? Like are you rich?"

Lionel snorted. "We don't need much."

I shook my head and tried to continue telling the truth as much as possible. "I have some money and I occasionally do a little work for people who need my help."

"I don't know what that means, but it sounds like you are in the mafia. Are you criminals?" I couldn't tell whether she thought that would be a bad thing.

"No. We aren't criminals. If we could show you a spell, it would help, but we need you to come with us for that." Lionel's frustration was evident.

"I have to be home soon. My foster parents get worried if I don't check in after school. I like it there and don't want to get moved to somewhere else. If I can stay there another two years, I'll be on my own." There was pain behind her words.

"Do you know of a place we can go where we'll have some privacy?" I hoped for something close, but I wasn't very confident.

"I can get out for a couple of hours after dinner. There's a place in Stanley Park I like to hang out. It's near the Malkin Bowl. We could meet there."

I guess she figured she could run if something went wrong. "Exactly where near the Bowl?"

She explained how to get to the clearing. "I get this weird feeling there. Weird but nice, like it's my home."

She was right to feel safe in that spot. It was an old gathering place for a group of air witches. Maybe her mother was one of them. The clearing was not far from the public path. And not far from help if she needed it. She was a smart girl.

"We'll meet you there in a couple of hours," I said.

"I'm bringing my friends," she announced. "I don't want to be there by myself."

"No," Lionel jumped in with the answer. "Your friends are not going to understand."

I glared at him. That was not the way to get her trust. "It would be best if they didn't come to watch us. If we are right, you'll come to understand why we don't like humans to know about us."

"Are you saying I'm not human?" Dionne said with an edge of panic. "You look human."

"We look human, but we can do magic, that means we aren't. I promise it will make sense when we confirm you are a witch." I needed her to believe before I could expose more of the Real Folk. I knew she was a witch, but she needed to know it. If she didn't believe, she might as well be human.

Lionel sighed. "I'm sorry. If you want to bring your friends, they can meet you after. If you bring them into the test, we'll have to change their memory and that can be a problem. It's hard to be accurate with that kind of spell."

"It will only take a half hour to finish the test. If you arrange to meet your friends at a coffee shop after that, it will mean someone will know where you are." If all went well, she would be back with her friends in plenty of time. And be anxious for our next meeting which would be in my house. There were too many curious Folk in the park for her to be safe as a newly discovered witch.

We sat sipping coffee while she talked herself into it. Eventually she said, "Okay. Seven, in the clearing. Don't try any funny stuff. I'm bringing mace." I heard her chair scrape as she stood. "See ya later," she called just before the doorbells tinkled behind her.

"Quinn, are you sure it's okay? Are you sure she's a witch?"

"Yes, she is. Let's get going. We have some arrangements to make. I think we should ask Beacon if he can drop by the clearing when we're finished testing her. He should be enough evidence that there's a different world right here."

CHAPTER 27

We were standing in the small clearing well before seven that evening. Lionel held the bag we'd filled with the items we needed for the tests. The air was chill, but I didn't want to attract attention, so we didn't start a fire.

A slight rustling of the dried ground cover caught my attention. "Hey, Quinn," Beacon said. "I got the message, but I can't come. I have to be across town at Trout Lake. Moss needs me to talk to the local fairies."

"Thanks, I'm sure we can call on a wood imp or fern fairy if necessary. I'll find a way to make sure they don't pull any tricks on her."

"No need," he said. "Moss will come by. He won't show himself until you call him. But I think he'll be a good example of Real Folk. And he's good with kids, so maybe he won't be too scary."

I hadn't had the nerve to ask Moss, but he would be perfect, and there was always a chance he had seen her before. And, come to think of it, he might know who her mother was. "Thanks, have fun with the Trout Lake gang. They can be a handful."

I didn't hear him leave, but I didn't expect to. "Lionel, you might as well lay out the charms and ingredients while we wait."

"Okay, but Quinn, it's getting dark, I think I should set a light for Dionne. I'll make it pale; I promise."

I nodded. She might not be able to see in the dark yet. And that made me worry what else she might know, or not know. My stomach had been churning acid for the last hour with waiting.

"How did you do that?" Dionne had come into the clearing without me hearing her. She could, at least, walk like a Real Folk.

"It's a simple spell," Lionel said. I remembered how frustrated he got during the week it took him to master it and smiled. "I can teach you this one first if the tests go well."

"Yeah, well it could be some hidden LED lights, so I'm not sure it's magic. It's not going to be that easy to convince me."

She was trying to sound worldly. Maybe her time in the foster system had made her more suspicious than I first realized.

"Thank you for coming, Dionne." I tried to set her at ease. "If you could come into the center of the clearing, Lionel is going to set a circle of power around us. When it's up, you'll see the outside as a bit blurry. Anyone coming up the path won't see the light; it will stay in the circle with us."

I held out my hand and she took it. I felt the vibration of her tension through the contact. I pulled her close so that Lionel could draw the circle tightly. It would be snug around the three of us, but we wouldn't need it long.

We sat on the ground and waited. I heard Lionel muttering the words that put power into the circle. He made it stronger than necessary, but that was probably for the best. "It's done," he whispered.

"Okay, Dionne, Lionel is going to do a little magic for you. Then we'll do two or three tests to see how strong your power is, and what kind of power you use. I know that you will have a lot of questions, but can you wait until we are done?"

"Yes," she breathed the word out. She was already more than halfway convinced.

"Lionel, go ahead."

We had agreed before coming that Lionel would create the image of her foster brother first. Then he would make flowers grow, and then fire. If that didn't bring her along, we were going to have to dig for deeper spells. He had a few charms in his pockets that would do, but they might cause a bit of a commotion.

I listened as he did his act.

"Oh my God, that's him. How are you doing that?" Dionne gasped. The scent of roses filled the circle and I dispelled it with a charm before it became overwhelming.

Then the circle warmed, and I heard a crackle of burning kindling. "Lionel, that feels a little too big."

"Sorry." He said the word to banish the flame.

"Dionne, are you satisfied that it's magic?" I could feel her amazement, but she needed to say it so she would believe it.

"I guess. Can you do other things? Could you make money out of magic?"

"No, at least not real money," Lionel said. "If we did it would be coins and by sunrise the next day it would be gone."

"Oh. So, what's next? You have to test me, right?" Now she sounded scared.

"It won't be hard, but first we need to figure out this glamour. Is there something you have with you all the time?" I really wanted that glamour. I'd replace it so she'd be safe, but I needed to trace that spell. It was our only lead to whoever turned her innocent spell into a deadly summoning.

"Um, yes. But it's something I had when I was left at the police station. I think it was from my mother."

"I won't take it away, but if you let me hold it for a minute, I can tell who set the glamour. Or, at least, I can make sure it won't interfere with the test." I hoped I would get what I needed, but no matter how much I wanted revenge, I couldn't take something that might belong to her mother.

"Okay, here." I held out my hand and she put a thin chain into it.

I felt a prickle of power, then a warm safe glow suffused my hand. A strong comfort spell was wrapped around the protective glamour. "Thank you. Give me a minute to figure this out, please."

I touched my senses to the spell. I expected to find it in tiny layers but there were only a few thin veneers on the original spell. This was a witch casting of love. Her mother had made the first glamour. It pulsed with life in my hands. This was no simple casting. This contained her mother's spirit. She must have done this as she died.

The upper layers of the spell were fairy work. They were more to check that the glamour held than to add any life to it.

I let my senses sink in further. An earth witch laid the spell. It didn't mean Dionne was an earth witch, but it would help find out who she was.

"Lionel, does Dionne look different?"

"No. Well, maybe she does a bit. Her hair is a bit lighter and her skin is fairer." He stuttered as he gave the description.

"Dionne, would you be okay if we left the chain on the ground while we tested you? You are safe in the circle."

She didn't respond right away and I started to think how to do the test through the protections. "I guess. It feels weird without it. I haven't taken it off before."

"It won't be long. Take my hands, please."

When she touched my palms, I was surprised how calm she was. Then I withdrew my probe and we only had physical contact. "I am going to try to reach your mind. I want you to keep me out. Just think about building a wall to keep me out."

I gave her a moment to prepare and then reached out to put my probe back. I slammed into a solid wall of NO!

She had protected herself well. She was strong, stronger than

Lionel, almost as strong as me. "Good. Now I want to try to identify what kind of witch you are. I need you to take down the wall."

"I felt you, but I don't know what you mean by take down the wall," she whispered. It didn't take a genius to realize she had stopped disbelieving and was only a tiny step away from believing.

"Breath in, then when you exhale imagine a brick wall falling." I hoped that would do it. My power was going to get a bruising if I had to go through the barrier.

I heard the breath and then felt the walls melt. She learned fast. I was going to have to find a strong teacher for her. "I am going to put some suggestions in your mind. I need you to tell me when you feel resonance."

"Okay, but what will that feel like?" She shifted and the wall in her mind wavered in and out of existence. I was going to have a headache when we were done.

"You might feel discomfort, or nothing, for everything that is wrong, but when I get the right thing, you'll feel like it fits."

She blew out a breath and said, "Okay. Go ahead I'm ready."

This test was simple. I imagined for her some spell casting based on the different types of witchery. An earth witch would use soil and since her mother was earth, I put a scene in her imagination of someone casting with mud. But she said nothing. The same with air, spirit, water and fire. By the time I got to fire, her walls were up again, and I couldn't convince her to drop them. Or rather, she couldn't drop them.

"I think that's enough for tonight, Dionne." I let go of her fingers. "Lionel, open the circle and let's see if Moss is there."

"But what about my magic?" Dionne sounded disappointed. Good, she believed.

"We'll find out another time. You need to get to your friends. And I have someone to introduce to you first." I held out the chain for her to take.

"Quinn Larson," Moss called.

"Just a second, Moss." I reached out and Dionne touched me again. "I want you to meet some of the other Real Folk. Dionne, there are so many others who inhabit our world. Moss is a sprite, and he tends the park. Don't be afraid."

"Hello," Moss spoke gently. "I am very pleased to meet you."

"Holy shit."

I laughed. "I guess I should have mentioned he was big."

I told Lionel to finish packing up our supplies while Moss told Dionne about the park. "What did you find out?" he asked.

"I'll tell you when we get home. How long has it been?"

"A half hour. You were right on time."

I asked him to take me to where the other two were talking. "I am sorry to break this up, but Dionne has to get to her friends before they worry. And we need to talk about where we'll meet next time."

"You come back when you want to talk to me," Moss said. "You can just say my name into the nearest bush or shrub, until you learn to see other Real Folk. I'll come when you call."

She said goodbye to Moss, and we started back towards the lights of the city. "So, what happens next? Do you teach me to do magic?"

"The next thing we do is meet. Will you come to my house now? I can promise it's more comfortable than the damp ground."

"Sure, where do you live?"

I gave her my address and we agreed she'd be there the next day after school. "I'll find you a teacher. Until I do, we can give you the basic lessons."

"Cool. I'm a witch."

I had a sudden picture of her playing witch and trying to turn her foster brother into a toad. "Promise me you won't try any magic on anyone."

"I promise, at least until I learn something. But when will you try to get my parents to talk to me?"

"We'll figure that out tomorrow. I need to learn more about

you. If I have to, I'll track down who your parents are, and we'll work from there."

"Okay." She kissed my cheek and left.

CHAPTER 28

The next afternoon, I felt my way downstairs to the workroom and sat on the bottom step. I wanted to do one more sweep of the room before Lionel returned from shopping and Dionne arrived. If there were any lingering spirits, they would affect the work we were going to do. And the news of a new witch would be racing through the city at the speed of gossip, if we let it slip. I didn't need every would-be teacher knocking on my door looking for a student. I needed to make sure she was put with the right teacher until she could become an apprentice.

I spread my power out into a thin sheet that filled the room like an inflated balloon. All surfaces were in contact with me. I looked for disturbances where the sense of me was mixed with something not me.

Only two places. One the center of the dirt floor where I called spirits and cast some of the more risky spells – and where Lionel did all of his work. The other was under the window.

A spider, just a normal one, was spinning her web at the bottom of the window. I sent a suggestion of cats in her direction and then chuckled as she skittered out through the gap she'd found behind the baseboard.

I stood and carefully found my way to the edge of the central pit. The place I'd left touching the earth. Someone was calling me. I couldn't let them through because I didn't have a way of containing them. Any circle I created was unlikely to be sealed, and unlikely to be a circle come to that.

Making sure nothing touched the earth to allow a conduit I sat on the edge of the step and pulled my balloon of power into a tent over the pit. "I am not available until midnight," I said.

A thin voice, maybe female, whispered back through the power. "It is urgent. I must speak before the girl comes."

"Voice only, and make it fast." Whoever it was could speak using my power tent but would not find access to this world through it.

"Fast is not a problem," the voice was stronger and definitely female. "You must not try to contact her mother or father."

"Wait. Not that fast. Why?" A feeling of gravity pushed at me. I wished Lionel was here to help bring this voice to a circle. Was this her mother, or the person who killed Dionne's parents, or Cate? Or someone really trying to help?

"I have less time than you have. When they find out I've been able to contact you, they may destroy what little is left of me. There are forces you do not want to disturb. Her parents disturbed them and now see what is happening."

The feeling of import was almost crushing me. "Can you tell me who they are?"

All that came in response was a scream.

CHAPTER 29

I sat there until Lionel called my name from the kitchen. There was no way I could refuse Dionne's request to call her parents to the circle without telling her there is danger. But I had no control over her until she became someone's apprentice. The apprentice oath constrained her from doing any magic without permission.

I had learned over the last few months with Lionel, to be sure to give him the go ahead when he'd learned a casting. But he was eager to be my apprentice. He knew from birth what he was, and he didn't have such a burning need for contact beyond death.

"Quinn, are you okay?" His voice was closer. "Oh, there you are. Look she'll be here soon. Should we go over the steps again? I don't want to get anything wrong."

I pushed myself up and felt my way to the door. While I'd been sitting, my power had returned to me and the room was clear. Now I had to decide whether to tell Lionel what had happened. If he knew he'd be able to help keep her distracted from a séance — I hated that word — and if he didn't, he couldn't let something slip by mistake.

"Put the kettle on and let's go over it again. You are right. This is more important than you think." I decided that I would tell him later.

"First, we tell her about the world of the Real Folk," I said as Lionel rustled about in the kitchen. "Just remember, Lionel, we don't want to overwhelm her."

"Yes, I can imagine what it will be like for her. I'll keep it to highlights." We had agreed that Lionel would do most of the talking for this part.

"Then we try to figure out what she is," I said it like it was a simple task. I wasn't used to going in blind, actually and metaphorically. There were a lot of tests we could try, but by her age most witches had found their calling. Until we knew what she was, no one could train her.

"I'll keep to our script until you tell me otherwise," Lionel said, sounding disappointed. "My job is to draw the circle and pass you anything you ask for. I've never drawn a circle around so much material. Are you sure it will work?"

We'd decided to make the circle as large as we could. I didn't want to have to stop because we'd forgotten an ingredient. So, the entire contents of my spell stores were inside the bare earth, along with about twenty books we could use for research.

"Yes. You are more than capable of casting the circle." I dragged my attention back to the present. "So, we run the same test as we did in the forest, just to be sure; earth, air, water, spirit and fire. Those are the most common because they are single focus."

"Then you'll go through them in combination." He sighed. "That's a lot of tests."

"We won't have to do them all. I'll follow trails. In the first set, one of the tests will be a bit more comfortable for her. I'll use that to prioritize the next set. Don't worry. We'll stop if we have to."

"Then you'll try to get her to agree to be apprenticed?" Lionel asked. "Do you know of any wizards or witches who will agree to part time training for two years?"

I hadn't even started that search. "No. Let's get her to agree first. Then we'll find someone. Just be honest about what it's like to apprentice. I want her to make an informed decision."

The door knocker interrupted whatever Lionel had to say.

CHAPTER 30

Dionne took the information about the Real Folk world pretty well, considering. We didn't fill in too many details because if we started, it would be hard to find a place to stop. She'd get that information from her teacher, and experience. And since only Beacon and Moss – and whoever kept up the glamour – knew she existed, we had some time.

An hour of testing had left us exhausted, and me with a pounding headache, again.

"I'm sorry we haven't been able to pinpoint it, Dionne," I said before running a final and unlikely test.

She gave the teenage sigh and said, "It's probably me. I just can't feel much difference between the images. Nothing feels wrong and nothing feels right."

"We need to clear out our minds before the last test. I don't want anything getting in the way. Dionne, let all the thoughts go. I'll know when you are done." We kept a light touch between us so I could place images in her mind. I'd been impressed at her ability to control her thoughts. Apparently foster children learn quickly to build defenses and hide their true feelings.

Her mind cleared in seconds, leaving behind only a slight tinge of anticipation. That would help her with the test. Lionel breathed out his thoughts and I let everything slip away except the test. The circle felt clean as though someone had swept it clear of the debris of our spells.

I started instructing Dionne, "I will place an image of you in your imagination. Around you will be elements of the four types of power. I want you to reach for the powers that mean the most to you." I'd saved this for the last test because she needed to take control, and I didn't know if she would be able to. And it required me to relinquish control. A level of trust I wasn't sure I had yet.

"Yes," she said, with no hesitation.

I pushed the image into her mind and waited. A small tug in my mind told me she was reaching for control. I let her take it. Within seconds, she sprouted four more arms and simultaneously picked up every single element.

I clutched at the earth to stop from shouting out, but I managed to end the test without jerking her back to reality.

"Wow, that was cool," she said. "I don't know how I did that. It just happened."

I gave her fingers a squeeze and then let go. "You did very well. Let's end the session and go back upstairs where we'll be more comfortable."

"What—" Lionel stopped his question as I cut him off with a flick of my hands.

"When we get upstairs. Now clear the circle."

He did it with speed and elegance. I felt a spike of pride. This was a spell he no longer needed me for.

When we were upstairs with the kettle boiling, I started to explain to Dionne what it meant to do as she had done. "You took control very easily. Without training, that already indicated you have strong powers. When you reached, as you did, for all of the elements, you showed that you are one of the rarest powers in our world. You have the ability to access any, and all, of the powers to do your magic."

Lionel gasped. "There is a legend that when we have six full powered wizards or witches, we will change the world. You are the third we know about."

"Can I meet them?" Dionne didn't seem at all awed about what we said.

I could have smacked Lionel for telling her. She needed to learn so much before she could manage the weight of prophesy. "They protect themselves. If one of them wishes to meet you it will happen. But until you have finished your apprenticeship, you will not find them."

"So how long is this apprenticeship? Like a year? I could do that."

I tried to get us back on the plan. As if following the steps we'd agreed to would somehow minimize the importance of our discovery. "Lionel, it might be a good time for you to tell her what it's like to be an apprentice."

"If you like to learn it's the best thing in the whole world. I had another master a while back, she died." His voice lost the rush of joy in the last sentence and I hoped he had the sense to move on. If Dionne knew what she'd done, I don't know how she'd react. "But Quinn is great. He trusts me with way more than she did."

"She," Dionne said. "You have female wizards?"

"No, sorry, I keep forgetting you don't know anything about us. witches and wizards are just the names. Women are witches and men are wizards. You can learn from either, and you don't need to learn from the same kind of power. The knowledge is the same. The difference is all in the way you apply it."

This wasn't the balanced view I was hoping for. "Lionel, tell her about the downside."

"Oh, yeah. You have to do a lot of chores, and you can't really ask why most of the time. I guess you can ask, but most of the time you don't get an answer. And you have to study all the time."

If that was his downside, maybe I was being too easy.

"So," Dionne said. "Who should I get to teach me? Or, I guess, who will you find to teach me?"

"I think Quinn should teach you." Lionel blurted out the words before I could even think of an answer.

"That would be great," she said, sounding like it was settled. "I could come here after school and on weekends and during breaks. I would need to think of something to tell the foster parents, but that should be easy. When do we start?"

I held up my hands to slow them down. "I have only had one apprentice since my own apprenticeship finished. I don't know if I can teach you. You have so much power and you will need to learn everything. We should find you someone more used to teaching." I was panicking, and that didn't bode well for a teacher.

"No, I trust you. And it's only for a year, right?" Hope brightened her voice.

"That depends." I realized Lionel hadn't cleared that up in his enthusiasm. "For most apprentices, it's four or five years. But they grew up in the world. You could be longer, or shorter, probably longer since you'll be part time for the first couple of years."

"Oh." I could hear the wheels turning as she planned how to speed up her learning time.

I continued, "Dionne, you will have to leave your friends behind. You'll have no time, and you'll constantly be struggling with what you can tell them and what you can't. You need the full attention of your teacher."

"Quinn?" Lionel apparently realized he may have said too much because he didn't often ask for permission to speak. I nodded and he continued. "I think we can do this. I can work with Dionne and I look her age so we could fake a normal relationship. Even though I'm pretty sure she's not much older than she looks."

I felt the pressure. They were ganging up on me. Maybe I could appeal to Lionel's need to learn. "Your own progress would slow down if you did that."

"I know, but I'm willing to have that happen. She is a full power. One of the six. We need to protect her as well as teach her. I am willing to give up that time."

I felt defeat wrap its arms around me. "Okay. But I need to know you'll listen to me. I need to trust that you won't teach her something I have refused to do."

"I willingly add that to my oath." Lionel's words were all it took to bind him.

I nodded and turned to where Dionne waited so patiently. "I need you to take an oath. It will bind you and there's no negotiating around the rules."

"Anything," she said and my link to her rang with the truth. This girl had found herself, and all doubts were gone for now. "Do you need blood? I will do anything."

I laughed, feeling a weight lift. Somehow, I knew this was the right thing to do. "No blood. We share a special tea that binds our words. You will swear to obey me during the time you are my apprentice. I will swear to teach you honorably and not hold you back. Normally an apprentice will swear to abide by the constraints of the power. With you that's a bit more complicated, so I'll ask you to swear to do no harm by action, or inaction. If you do that, you will still be able to cast any spell I give you in a protective circle, but it won't work at all if a human is present."

"Okay, make the tea. I'm ready."

We did the ceremony and Dionne gave her oath truly.

"Now you go home. I want you back here on Saturday, ready to spend the whole day with us. Be here by nine am."

"I'll tell my foster parents that I'm volunteering to clean up a river or something. I'll make it a weekend activity." She kissed my cheek again and left.

"We'll have to stop the kissing," Lionel said. "It's not appropriate."

I chuckled and said, "Let's go to Banks'. I need a hearty meal and a beer. We have three days to figure out how to protect her while introducing her to the Real Folk."

WANT MORE?

What can Dionne's power mean to Quinn's world? Use the QR code to grab your copy of Obsession and discover the prophecy.

Sneak peek next.

If you enjoyed reading Compulsion, please consider helping other readers to find the story by leaving a review.

※ I ※

I t was Saturday, and it was going to be Dionne's first full day with us. Lionel was up early. By the smell of bleach and vine- gar, he must have cleaned the house before I got up. As soon as I had my breakfast in front of me, he said, "I'm going for groceries. If Dionne's going to be here all day, we can't expect her to live off tea and oatmeal."

I dug into the pocket of my jeans for money and handed him a wad of bills. As his footsteps echoed from the hall, I realized I'd need to generate more income if I was going to be supporting two teenagers. Just another detail in the complexity of my new life. I made most of my money through on-line ads that I'd set up before I lost my sight. I'd been surprised how easy it was to lace a spell through the internet. I never compelled people to buy, just to click. That's all it took to keep enough money going to my account to pay the bills. And it didn't take much power from me to keep the spell running.

The problem wasn't really the money. No matter how much I tried to ignore it, the real problem was Dionne. I'd never trained a witch before, other wizards trained witches and wizards alike. My only experience was Lionel, and I'd inherited him from Cate. On top of that, Dionne was one of the six wizards with five powers who would bring about a prophecy that no one seemed to understand.

As if that wasn't bad enough, she'd grown up among the humans and didn't know she was a witch until we tested her.

"Hello, Quinn?" Dionne called from the door. "Are you there?"

I realized that in the rush after her test I hadn't given her access through the wards. "Come in, I'm in the kitchen." That would give her access to the main floor. Later, I could put some layers on the workshop to restrict her in the same way Lionel wasn't able to access everything down there.

While she came down the hall, I added a quiet restriction to stop her from inviting people in without Lionel or me present. I didn't want to come home one day to find a party raging in the living room.

She plunked down in the chair next to mine. "I'm yours until eight. I couldn't get the foster parents to buy that I'd be cleaning a river after dark. I told them I was having dinner with friends. We should probably introduce Lionel as my friend soon. How are you?"

I laughed. This was going to be interesting, not easy, but definitely interesting. "I'm fine. Lionel will be back in a few minutes. Make yourself comfortable."

"No. I'm good," she said. "Listen, I had an idea last night. Maybe you can pretend to be my uncle. If you did, I would be able to move in here. Then everything would be better."

I heard Lionel come in as I tried to marshal an argument. From a learning point of view, it would be much better if she was living here. From a peace of mind point of view, I wasn't sure I was ready to have a chattering teenage girl around all the time. And purely logistically, there wasn't a free bedroom. We'd have to clear a room in the attic, and I wasn't able to do the renovation spell it would require because I couldn't see. And I didn't know if I should trust Lionel with it. "Wouldn't the authorities need a lot of proof before handing you over to an uncle?" I asked, hoping human bureaucracy would come to my rescue.

"Yeah there would be paperwork, but we could make it right with magic. We could use a spell to convince them." She'd obviously been giving this a lot of thought. My guess was she'd been wishing for an uncle or aunt to show up for years.

I hated to flatten her hopes, but I didn't need the intrusion of whatever government agency looked after foster children. "I don't think that's a good idea because there's probably a lot of checks and balances. It would be a very complex spell. And—"

"But we could do it." She trampled over my words.

"We could at least try to find out," Lionel chipped in. "It would be better for her to get full time training. I mean it's going to take months just to get her to understand the world we live in."

"See, Lionel agrees with me," Dionne said.

I shook my head. "Nice try. He doesn't agree with you, but he has a point. We'll see what it would take. But I need to know a lot more about your parents first. If I'm an uncle, I should be able to tell someone about them. I don't even know what they looked like."

"There are pictures you can look at." Her voice was suddenly quiet.

"You have pictures?" That would go a long way to helping solve the mystery of who she was, but Lionel would have to be my eyes, as usual.

I heard a little catch in her breath before she spoke again. "No, I don't. The pictures are of the crime scene. The police have them. I can get them if you like, but I don't think I can look at them."

I didn't need my sight to know she was fighting tears.

I wanted to pat her shoulder but wasn't willing to take the chance of what I would end up touching. "We'll start by figuring out how to get the files from the police. Then we'll talk about moving you here. But right now, we need to put you under a new glamour."

"Why?" Her interest was back, and I let myself believe I'd dodged the bullet of her living arrangements for now.

"We're going to take you to Banks' pub for lunch," Lionel said.

"I'm too young to go to a pub," she said.

"You can go into this one. No one will be the wiser, at least no human. Real folk don't care how old you are as long as you don't disturb the relative peace. Even so, you'll be drinking tea or coffee. I'm not sending you back to your foster parents with alcohol on your breath." I paused to let her react, but she didn't say anything, so I continued, "The glamour will change your appearance slightly. Just enough so no one will recognize you. The Real Folk will notice your appearance has been altered, but everyone occasionally adds or subtracts a bit from their looks. No one will be suspicious."

"Cool," she said. "Will it be enough to stop people who know me really well recognizing me? Like I would hate to have someone tell the foster parents they saw me downtown when I was supposed to be in Richmond."

I was going to have to break her of the habit of adding 'like' into her conversations. Preciseness of language was a vital component of successful spell casting. "Yes, it will hide you from people you know."

"Can I be a redhead? A tall redhead? I've always wanted to be tall and glamorous."

I nodded and directed her down to the workroom. "Lionel will do the glamour. It will be good practice for him. And while he does, I'll start your lessons with the history of the world."

I heard a groan from both of them. Lionel was still struggling to get his glamours right, despite his success with Beacon, and Dionne was probably expecting a dry list of battles and knights. I suppressed a chuckle. "When I'm satisfied your glamour is complete, Lionel, we'll go. I have a mirror down here somewhere that Dionne can look in to see what you've done."

It took two hours for Lionel to get the look Dionne wanted, because she kept asking for just a little more, and I wouldn't step in to say no. I could feel the power of the spell settle and it would be enough to deflect any Real Folk from looking too deeply and seeing her powers. My quick summary of the world as we know it had grabbed Dionne's interest and I was encouraged to think she'd be as good a student as Lionel.

We left to go to Banks' for lunch, and I was looking forward to her reaction to the full gamut of Real Folk.

WE STAYED FOR LUNCH AND ENOUGH TIME FOR LIONEL AND ME to enjoy a couple of beers while Dionne did her best to sound cool without missing anything that was going on. She'd been chattering all the way back to the house. "That was cool, can we go back? I want to talk to everyone again." She was buzzing with energy.

I released some of the wards on my workroom and waved her ahead of me. "Yes, but we need to spend some time on your training."

She kept up a running commentary as we made our way down the few steps and across to the center of the bare earth. Lesson learned for me, never start the day with a trip to Banks'.

I heard the door close and Lionel clomp down to join us. "Wait until you see it on a busy day," he said. "You didn't even get to meet any kobolds or sidhe. That was weird, Quinn. I wonder why the sidhe weren't there."

I felt really old compared to with the energy radiating off the two of them. "I don't know, Lionel. Before we worry about that, how about we give Dionne some more of the history of the Real Folk?"

"Great idea," Lionel said.

Dionne groaned. "Can't we just start with some spells? If there's a history book, I can take it home and read it. Or if we have to do research, why not start with my prophecy?"

I ignored the whine building in her voice. "Spells will come later. Unless you want to just stay here for lessons and not meet other people? Not go to Banks'? We'll get to the prophecy soon."

"Why not now?"

I could almost feel the pout that must be on her face. "I need to figure out how to approach the investigation. It's complicated, Dionne."

"Okay, fine. But does it have to be all the history? Like, can we just go over the high points? Then maybe some spells?" She paused. "Or, maybe you can tell me what you know about the prophecy. Maybe that will give us a clue how to start."

It was a reasonable question. I just didn't have any information for her. "We'll start with some history. If we have time, I'll talk about the prophecy." And maybe I would have some idea what to say when we got to it.

"Yes, we have to think about what we know," Lionel said. "I have to warn you, Dionne, there isn't much information."

She sighed, and I held back a wince. I'd broken Lionel of that habit, and now I would have to start again. "Okay, no problem," she said, bouncing back with all the energy of a teenager. "So, am I going to have to memorize a bunch of dates? Battles and stuff?"

I laughed. "No, it's more about the stories of the Real Folk, the magical people. How they arrived here, their power, their weaknesses. And the threat they pose."

"You'll like it. Like Quinn said, it's stories." Lionel put something on the bench and added, "Shall I make tea?"

We'd already burned half the day at Banks' and needed to get on with the lessons. "Maybe later. A couple of hours of history and then we'll have a break."

"Why do we have to work down here?" Dionne asked from

somewhere near the window. "It would be more comfortable upstairs. And there'll be more light."

"Yes, but it's more private down here." I pointed toward where the couch had been last time. "Have a seat."

Her footsteps stopped. "Why do we need privacy?" There was fear in her voice. Something that I hadn't heard in all the times we'd talked before. She'd always been in control, even when she'd met us in the park.

"I want Lionel to cast some images for you," I said. "Why are you worried?"

"I'm not. So, let's get on with it."

I decided to let it go. She would tell me eventually. "Okay, let's get settled."

I had Lionel create images of the kobolds to start with, and then told him to explain their powers and weaknesses. I had learned the value of getting two things done at the same time when I first took on Lionel as an apprentice.

After Lionel had recited the kobold descriptions, I said, "The sidhe are more complicated, but Lionel can give you the run down on the structure of the court, and then we'll put off the rest until later."

"Quinn," Lionel said. "I've been thinking. Maybe we should look at the facts we know about the prophecy."

Didn't either of them understand the relationship between master and apprentice? I was going to have to work hard to stay in control.

"Yeah, that would be good," Dionne said. "I can learn this other stuff later."

"Let's see how well you learned the kobolds before we stop the lessons." I sympathized with her. She had been living a lie all of her life. I could sympathize with Lionel too. This was all stuff he knew. Bringing Dionne into her birthright shouldn't stall his training, but it would. All I could do was let him teach as much as possible, at least that would reinforce his training.

It was time to start the quiz. "Dionne, name three characteristics of the kobold that points to their heritage."

Another sigh introduced the answer. "They are armored. This shows they developed in a place that could have caused them damage. They are strong, meaning their environment was harsh. They are capable of disguising themselves, meaning they lived, or traveled, among humans."

She had done a good job of synthesizing the facts that Lionel had given her. "You have a good memory. I think we can limit ourselves to a couple of species a visit."

"So, we can talk about the prophecy?"

"No," I said. Hearing two people take in a breath to argue, I held up my hand. "Just listen. Lionel and I need to do more research before we talk about it. I promise we won't keep anything from you."

"I can do some research tonight," Lionel said.

"Can I help?" Dionne asked. "I'm good at research. I always get great marks on my projects."

I'd talk to Lionel later to get him to slow down and maybe get him to take my side in these situations. He needed to help get Dionne trained before we let her get into prophecies. "Let's move onto sprite folklore and then we'll break for a snack."

W e were gathered at the counter, tea and blueberry scones fortifying us, for the next part of the lessons. I was going to teach Dionne to boil water. Well, Lionel would teach her with me listening to the instructions.

The doorbell rang as I was explaining the theory of the spell. "Lionel, go see who that is. Dionne, please go into my bedroom until we know it's safe." The last thing we needed was for someone to find one of the six before she was ready.

Dionne took her tea and pastry with her.

The bell rang again before Lionel got to it. I heard a high piping voice and Lionel's rumble. Princess – Great! The bringer of many problems.

I knew Lionel would limit her access to the house, but she was sneaky. I would have to trust him to keep an eye on her while she visited. I waited until they joined me before acknowledging her. "Princess, it's a delight to have you in my home."

"I know, Quinn Larson." She touched my hand and I felt the dryness of her skin. Princess was getting old. "You still cannot see, is that correct?"

"I have not found the cure for Fionuir's spell, no."

"Then I must tell you that I have brought my eldest daughter with me today. I must ask you for a favor."

"What do you need from me?"

"First, let me introduce my child. Quinn Larson, this is Bud, my child and heir. She will rule the Rose tribe when I am gone."

"A long time from now I hope?" I held out a hand low to the ground. "It is good to meet you, Bud." I felt the touch of tiny fingers.

"I've never met a wizard before. How do you cast spells if you can't see?" Bud's voice was barely audible it was so high in pitch.

"I manage. Can I offer you anything? Perhaps some honey?" I had lost track of Lionel. I hoped he was monitoring Princess. The last time she came to ask for a favor, or told me she would do me a favor by allowing me to find her treasure, she'd tried to drop enough beads in my house to grant her access regardless of my wards.

"I do not have time today for your hospitality," Princess said. "I need you to train Bud to be a leader."

"What makes you think I could do that? I have little knowledge of fairy politics." And I really didn't have time to train anyone else.

Princess gave a sigh that rivaled Dionne's efforts. I was going to have to cast a no sighing spell on the house before it drove me mad.

"See mother, I told you I didn't need training."

"Bud, be quiet. I know what you need. I am the queen, and you will obey me." Princess snapped her fingers. "Now, Quinn Larson, it is not lessons in politics I ask for. She is lacking in compassion. I worry that she will become a poor leader."

I couldn't bring Bud into my house. Dionne needed me more than Princess, and too many people around meant too big a chance her secret would come out. "There are other people who can do a much better job at teaching her than I can."

"No. You are the best teacher. Lionel is a much better wizard, and man, than he was. You have taken time to teach him more than magic."

I should know better than to try to argue with Princess. I hadn't won an argument yet, but I had to try. "I didn't want an apprentice, Princess, you know that. I only took him on because I owed Cate. I'm not taking on another one."

"I hear you have already taken on another. This girl you brought into Banks' this morning. Dionne, is that her name?"

Damn. "Yes, that's her name. So, you can see, for a wizard who wanted no apprentices, I have enough to keep me busy."

"Bud is small. She will not take up much of your time." Princess was not going to let me off the hook. "If you train her well, you will not have to help the fairies again, perhaps."

"That's a big perhaps, Princess. Have you done something to my apprentice?"

"He is held at the door by a charm. I will free him when I leave. I did not wish him to witness my embarrassment." Her voice didn't carry any tinge of embarrassment. She'd frozen Lionel to show me she still had the power; or maybe to prove it to herself.

It was time to try another tack. "If I were to agree, there would be conditions." There had to be something she wouldn't agree to.

"I expected as much. Tell me them so we can be done. I am tiring."

I thought for a moment. If I lost the negotiation, there was one thing I needed in place to ensure Dionne's safety. "I need her to take the apprentice oath. I have things I do not wish made public."

"I can keep secrets," Bud squeaked from behind me.

Princess hissed. "I said to be quiet. You see what I must put up with, Quinn Larson. She will take your vow. What else?"

This was too easy. "She will be here at nine every day and will do as we ask. She will take orders from me, and my apprentices, without argument."

Princess laughed, a rising tinkle of sound that ended in a gasp for air. She was really coming to the end of her life. "If you can get her to agree to the last part of that, you truly are a great teacher. I will ensure she is here on time. Is there anything else?"

I conceded. "No, we'll start tomorrow."

I felt a touch on my hand. "Thank you, Quinn. This is the most important favor you have done for me. Until tomorrow."

"Tomorrow. Don't forget to release Lionel."

She laughed again. "Your lack of sight is not a problem for your memory, I see. I will not forget to release him, and he will not be hurt. You will need him when my child comes for her lessons." She patted my hand. "Bud, come along. Tomorrow you can take your oath."

"Princess, be well. I would not like to lose you before Bud is trained."

A featherlike kiss landed on my cheek. "I would not let that happen to my tribe."

A few seconds later, Lionel stomped back into the kitchen. "I heard everything. You are getting a reputation for teaching, Quinn. Maybe we should look into those renovations. Maybe we can turn the attic into bedrooms and open a school. This is so cool."

"Let's get back to teaching Dionne while we only have her to worry about." I called the girl back to the kitchen.

BY THE TIME WE'D FINISHED OUR SNACK, DIONNE HAD THE theory for the water boiling spell down pat. We were just getting ready to head down to the workroom when the doorbell rang again.

"We are popular today," I said gesturing to Dionne to go back into my bedroom. "We'll both go to the door this time, Lionel. You stand back with a repel spell just in case someone tries the same thing as Princess did. We can't be spending time waiting for freeze spells to pass." I heard my bedroom door close and turned to the front hall.

"Quinn, let me look through the peephole. No one can cast through the house wards. When we know who's there, we can be better prepared."

I gave him a little push so he was ahead of me. I was so used to my blindness that I sometimes forgot I couldn't do everything I used to. "Don't open the door until I tell you."

It felt a bit like we were defending my house from attackers. But if Princess was able to cast a spell on my apprentice, I wasn't willing to chance what a stranger would do.

"It's three druids," Lionel said in awe.

Druids; this day was not getting better. "Okay, let them in with restrictions to this floor." I started back to the living room. I might as well get comfortable.

I heard Lionel chatting, but the druids didn't speak to him. I couldn't understand why he seemed to revere them when they ignored him.

"Quinn Larson," a dry voice announced.

"Yes." I wasn't going to give them any help.

"You have done us a service in the past. We require you to do one more thing." The voice came from beside me, this time. I was used to that. All druids either sounded the same, or made themselves sound that way, to outsiders.

"You require? I have no obligation to you."

"We will not accept denial of our request."

"Requests do not come as requirements." I didn't know how badly they wanted this thing, but I wanted time to train my apprentices in peace. If insulting them would make the druids go away, I'd take the chance.

There was a dry rustle of whispers. Then they turned their attention back to me. "Perhaps our choice of words was unfortunate. We have a problem and believe you are the solution."

I felt Lionel settle beside me on the couch. The druids had promised to teach him when he was ready, and he knew better than to risk their goodwill. If he kept silent, he wouldn't put that in jeopardy no matter what I said or did.

"What is your problem?"

"Then you agree to do us this service?"

"No, I am curious to know what you need. I may choose to help if you are willing to negotiate for my time."

"You must free the sidhe Fionuir from the dimensional fold in which you have her prisoner."

That was a surprise. I knew Fionuir would have to be freed eventually. I wasn't stupid enough to think I could keep her there forever. I had hoped it would be done by someone else long after I was gone. And if I had to release her before that, I would need a lot of protection. "I'll ignore your choice of words. Why do you need her freed?"

"Why is not important. We require this of you."

I reminded myself that patience is a virtue, and that the druids would never change their demanding approach. They would tell me what I needed to know if they wanted to, and if I asked the right questions. "I do not wish to obstruct your plans but releasing her is not my sole discretion. I believe Queen Maeve will want some power in that decision. And there are others who Fionuir may feel compelled to punish for her imprisonment. I am happy to carry your message, but I need to know why you wish her freed. If I know that, I can plead your case."

There were whispers for a few minutes before the druid on my left spoke again. "We are also constrained by other concerns, which we do not wish to share with you."

"I will keep your secrets. I cannot convince Queen Maeve

without information." Maybe a reminder of her stature would help them bend.

"We cannot simply provide information. Before we consider sharing more, tell us if it is possible to release Fionuir."

"Yes, I can bring her back to this dimension. I have created alternate avenues for doing so in the event I am unable." Clarence had one spelled charm and Olan the other. Neither would use them unless they knew I was dead. "Before you ask, I will not tell you what those alternate avenues are."

"It is not important. Signs point to you as the person who imprisoned her. You must be the one to free her."

"What signs?" I was just about done with their secrecy.

There was whispering again, and then the voice came from my right this time, "The souls in the Gur amulet are stirring."

That wasn't good. The Gur amulet contained the souls of murdered druids. If they were stirring... well it wouldn't be good news. "What makes you think that has anything to do with Fionuir?"

"We cannot say, but we will ask the council if we can share any information. It would be helpful to give them assurance that you will free her. It is important that the souls remain at rest. Even Queen Maeve will not be happy with the results if they should be more disturbed."

"I cannot give you those assurances without conditions." I was beyond tired of this. We were wasting the little time we had of Dionne's day. There was nothing in my bedroom to teach her, but there was no way I was letting her out in front of the druids. I'd keep her secret from them as long as possible. If they knew they had access to one of the six, they wouldn't leave her alone, and we would be overrun with creepy guys in black robes and hoods. My neighbors would start to suspect I was not normal – for a human anyway.

The rustling stopped. A voice came from the far side of the room. "Name your conditions."

I felt Lionel shifting on the couch beside me and figured he wanted me to include some more training time with the druids. I ignored the command in the voice. "I must have Maeve's approval. Fionuir is her subject, and I am not interfering with sidhe politics."

"It seems you have already done that by imprisoning Fionuir," a dry voice said. "Or perhaps you were acting on Maeve's orders?"

I wasn't going to gossip about the sidhe Queen. "Maeve did not order me to get rid of Fionuir." Well, not actually, but she wasn't unhappy about it when I sent her rival away.

"Very well, are there any other conditions you wish to place on the peace of our murdered brothers' souls?"

"No more conditions, but I will require compensation. I will be taking a risk by freeing her. Fionuir will not be happy about her imprisonment." That was an understatement. She'd make my life a living hell, and I'd be lucky if she didn't kill me.

"We cannot agree to payment, but we will take your price to the council. I would not ask for too much, wizard."

I'm not sure why they didn't come prepared. Did they assume I would just agree to the request to free her? "You owe Lionel a month of training. I would have that extended to two months. In addition, I have need of information."

"We hold much knowledge in our library. Anyone is welcome to research any topic they desire while in there."

That was true, but nothing was indexed. Or more accurately the index wasn't made available to non-druids, and there was a magic dampening spell cast across the whole building. "I do not wish to spend my life trying to find the information I seek. The price, if I agree to release her, is to receive the information directly."

"Perhaps the council will agree to that. What is this information?"

"I will tell you that when we have an agreement. Now, I have an apprentice to train. Is there anything else we need to discuss before you can speak to your council?"

I heard a rustle of fabric and felt Lionel rise. "We will return after speaking to the council. Be prepared to act when we next meet. You will get approval from Maeve while you wait for the council's decision."

"Yes, I think it's best that we deal with this as quickly as possible." Their attitude had pushed my courtesy to the edge. "Perhaps it is time for you to do your part."

Lionel showed them out, and by the time he got back, Dionne was in the kitchen. "If I have to keep hiding in there every time someone comes over, can you keep something interesting for me to do? Like, your computer or something?"

"I hope we won't be interrupted again today, but that's a good idea. Lionel can sort out some history books for you to study." The groan I heard did not surprise me. "Let's get you working on the water spell before you have to leave."

DIONNE MANAGED TO GET SOME STEAM RISING FROM A VERY small cup of water before she left. I had expected her to be frustrated at the slow progress, but she was cheerful with what she had accomplished. We were still working out her schedule, but she promised to try to come by for at least part of the day tomorrow. I worried that if we couldn't work full days on weekends, we'd be forever getting her trained.

Now, Lionel was digging through some of my older texts for hints about the prophecy, and I fully expected he would be there all night. It was getting close to midnight and my mind was restless with the day's events. I made a mug of calming tea and went to the back garden to attempt to sort everything out.

It was still warm enough in the evenings to enjoy the night air. I maintained a spell over the house, and my neighbors to keep the mosquitoes at bay, so it was always comfortable in the garden. I sank back in one of the wicker chairs and imagined the night sky. The moon would be almost full but hidden behind the towers a few blocks away.

One of my neighbors was still up, a faint murmur of music drifting across the lane. The gentle noise was better for my mood than silence would have been. I sent my senses out further, hearing the whisper of traffic on Burrard Street. A sudden scream of an ambulance siren startled me back to myself. Living so close to St. Paul's hospital was the only downside of the neighborhood.

I sipped the tea and felt the calm from the herbs flow through my body. A deep breath took my cares out on the exhale. Things would work out. Having Bud in the house would help Dionne, who was feeling the gap between Lionel's knowledge and her own. Although she hadn't mentioned it, I could feel it in every sigh and silence.

If the druids met my conditions, and Maeve could contain her, I'd be happy to free Fionuir. I knew we had no choice but to put her there when she attacked us. I didn't like to leave her in the dimensional fold. People went mad in such isolation.

"Quinn, are you not aware of me? Or are you ignoring me?" The voice was warm, and soft, and welcoming.

I spilled tea on my lap. "Damn, how did you get there without me noticing?"

"Language, Quinn," The Morrigan said, her voice now more like a crow and carrying a clear warning.

"Sorry, you startled me. It is good to see you, so to speak."

I felt warm flesh press against my arm. Even without sight, I felt the raw sexuality of her fertility aspect. It became hard to breathe, and then the flesh turned into feathers, and the chill of death replaced the heat of sex. I wanted to ask her to stay in crow form, it was less distracting, but I'd already crossed a line, so I kept my mouth shut.

"I forgive you, this time."

"Is this a social visit?"

"It is not. I have come to warn you. The thing I have been sensing is approaching. Something is changing the fate of this world."

Despite the fact I could feel her warm skin against my arm again, she sounded angry enough to peck my eyes out.

So much for the idea of relaxing before I went to bed. I'd thought she was omniscient. It was disconcerting to think that there was something that she could only sense. "Do you have any idea what it is?"

I heard a caw and felt the life drain from me. "No, I do not!" She switched back to woman and life flowed back into my body on a warm silky breeze. "It is not usual that something should be hidden from me. It is normal for me to choose what to tell and what to keep hidden. I am not happy about this situation, Quinn Larson."

I didn't know what to say. How did one comfort the goddess of death and life? "I'm sure you will know before any of us."

A beak clacked. "It doesn't matter. I will feed on the aftermath either way."

I was weary of the tension that long encounters with The Morrigan brought. Not knowing whether I would be filled with grief or lust – and getting both – frayed my nerves. "Is there something I can do for you?" I hoped not. I had enough on my plate.

"Yes." The warmth of my first love flowed with the word. "Be careful. I think this thing is aimed at you. Or perhaps someone close to you."

"You care about me?" Was that a good thing?

"I care about all creatures. I am there at their creation and at their destruction." The pain of birth and battle death filled my mind. "But yes, Quinn, you interest me. I am not ready to take your spirit, yet."

A flap of wings and an icy breeze stopped my next question. She was gone. The night warmed and the scent of jasmine from my garden replaced a whiff of death.

WHAT CAN DIONNE'S POWER MEAN TO QUINN'S WORLD? USE the QR code to grab your copy of Obsession and discover the prophecy.

FREE EBOOK

Claim your copy of Spells and Other Charms when you use the QR code to sign up for my newsletter and learn more about Quinn and Cate's past.

ALSO BY P A WILSON

For more books by P A Wilson
Use the QR code below or go to pawilson.ca

ABOUT THE AUTHOR

Perry Wilson is a Canadian author based in Vancouver, BC who has big ideas and an itch to tell stories. Having spent some time on university, a career, and life in general, she returned to writing in 2008 and hasn't looked back since (well, maybe a little, but only while parallel parking).

She is a member of the Vancouver Writers Social Group, The Royal City Literary Arts Society, and The Surrey Writing Workshop. Perry has self-published several novels. She writes the Madeline Journeys, a fantasy series about a high-powered lawyer who finds herself trapped in a magical world, the Quinn Larson Quests, which follows the adventures of a wizard named Quinn who must contend with volatile fae in the heart of Vancouver, and the Charity Deacon Investigations, a mystery thriller series about a private eye who tends to fall into serious trouble with her cases, and The Riverton Romances, a series based in a small town in Oregon, one of her favorite states. Her stand-alone novels are Breaking the Bonds, Closing the Circle, and The Dragon at The Edge of The Map.

For more information
www.pawilson.ca
pawilson@pawilson.ca

 X

ACKNOWLEDGMENTS

People think that the process of writing is solitary. That's not the case for me. I have help from so many people it would be hard to acknowledge everyone, but I'll give it a try.

The support and inspiration I get from my writer's groups is incalculable. The Vancouver Writers Social Group opens my mind to other ways of telling a story. The Royal City Literary Arts Society gives me the opportunity to meet and share with other writers who have more knowledge than I do. The Other 11 Months group is where I learn about getting the words on the page. And my critique group who helps me find the best parts of the story I want to tell. Thanks to all of the members of these great groups.

Last of all, but definitely a huge part of the process, my beta readers. These are the people who love stories and are willing, and more than able, to tell me if my finished story is ready for you, my readers.